THE SWARMS RECKONING

Larry Brower

The Silent War

THE AWAKENING FURY

The air itself was a chemical shroud, a testament to humanity's unending war. Generations had passed since the spraying began, a relentless deluge of synthetic doom designed to scour the planet clean of its most numerous inhabitants. For the colossal beings who called themselves humankind, it was a necessary sanitation, a sterile victory over the buzzing, crawling, and biting masses. But for the insect kingdoms, it was slow, agonizing annihilation.

Fields that once pulsed with the vibrant hum of life were now silent, their soil leached and sterile. The verdant tapestry of forests, once teeming with a thousand shades of green and the myriad lives they harbored, had thinned into skeletal specters. Where pollinators had once danced in a symphony of life-giving dust, now only the sterile wind whispered through brittle stalks. The very essence of growth was being choked, poisoned by the invisible tendrils of neonicotinoids, organophosphates, and a cocktail of other arcane compounds churned out in human factories. These were not mere inconveniences; they were weapons of mass destruction, deployed with a casual indifference that spoke volumes of humanity's perception of their own species' dominance.

Within the hives, a different kind of battle raged. For the honeybees, keepers of ancient floral knowledge and architects of intricate, waxen cities, the poison was a pervasive enemy that seeped into the very nectar they collected. Each drop of tainted sweetness, each grain of contaminated pollen, was a seed of destruction planted within their colonies. The once-robust larvae, the future of their lineage, succumbed to internal hemorrhages, their tiny bodies wracked with tremors that mimicked the earth's quakes. Queens, the very heart of the hive, grew sluggish, their pheromonal whispers weakening, unable to guide their workers with the clarity that had ensured survival for millennia. The hum of the hive, once a constant thrum of industry and life, had become a mournful drone, punctuated by the rasping breaths of the dying. Colonies withered from within, their meticulously constructed honeycombs becoming mausoleums of unfulfilled potential.

The fire ants, masters of subterranean engineering and tenacious survivors, fared little better. Their vast, interconnected networks of tunnels, stretching for miles beneath the surface, became death traps. The very earth, saturated by relentless aerial assaults of toxic dust, leached the poison into their carefully regulated chambers. Ants that ventured to the surface to forage were met with a swift, agonizing paralysis, their segmented bodies convulsing before life drained away, leaving them as brittle, dessicated husks. Those who remained below, breathing air filtered through poisoned soil, developed internal lesions, their haemolymph turning viscous and dark. Even their formidable reproductive capabilities faltered as generations of chemical exposure led to widespread sterility and developmental deformities. The fierce, unyielding spirit that had characterized their species was being systematically eroded, replaced by a pervasive weariness.

The killer bees, their venom a precise and lethal instrument, found their own efficacy blunted by the ubiquitous chemicals. While their stings remained potent against their natural prey, the lingering residues on flowers and foliage rendered their food sources toxic. Their tireless flights, once a testament to their dedication, became perilous journeys into poisoned territories. Many returned to the hive not with nectar, but with the deadly particles clinging to their wings and bodies, inadvertently contaminating the shared stores and spreading the insidious sickness. The frenzied dances that communicated the location of bountiful flowers became dances of despair, leading their sisters to death instead of sustenance. The very act of survival was now a pathway to extinction.

Even the apex predators of the insect world, the formidable murder hornets, felt the insidious touch of humanity's chemical warfare. Their preferred prey, the very creatures they so efficiently dispatched, were themselves weakened and deformed by the pesticides. A hornet that consumed a diseased caterpillar or a contaminated beetle carried the poison within its own formidable frame. While their hardened exoskeletons offered some initial protection, the cumulative effect of this bioaccumulation began to manifest. Their powerful mandibles, capable of slicing through chitin and flesh, grew less efficient, their venom glands less potent. A subtle lethargy began to creep into their decisive strikes, a creeping weariness that was utterly alien to their nature. The fear they instilled in other creatures was slowly being replaced by a dawning, primal dread of their own kind.

The landscape bore the grim scars of this silent war. Once-lush meadows, where wildflowers had bloomed in a riot of color, were now patchy expanses of brown and yellow. The vibrant greens of the canopy had faded, replaced by a sickly pallor, the leaves brittle and prematurely shed. Rivers and streams, once crystal arteries of life, often ran with unnatural hues, reflecting the runoff from fields and the effluence from industrial sites that produced the very agents of destruction. The smell of rain, once a promise of renewal, now carried the acrid tang of chemical residue, a constant reminder of the pervasive contamination.

The silence was the most chilling aspect. The cacophony

of buzzing, chirping, and fluttering that had defined the natural world for eons was being systematically silenced. Birdsong was more muted, the insects they fed upon scarce. The rustle of leaves was no longer accompanied by the frantic scuttling of beetles or the determined march of ants. A profound emptiness was settling over the land, a void where a vibrant, interconnected ecosystem had once thrived. This was not a sudden, cataclysmic event, but a slow, inexorable decay, a creeping death that had seeped into the very fabric of life.

For generations, the insect kingdoms had endured this systematic extermination. They had witnessed the slow demise of their kin, the barrenness of their ancestral foraging grounds, the contamination of their water sources. Instinct, honed over millions of years, screamed of danger, of an existential threat unlike any they had faced before. Yet, their responses had always been individual, localized, a desperate attempt to survive within the suffocating grip of humanity's chemical dominion. They retreated, they adapted where they could, but the sheer scale and persistence of the assault overwhelmed their innate resilience.

But something was changing. The very agents of their near-annihilation, the relentless barrage of toxins, were, in a twisted irony, becoming catalysts for an unprecedented evolution. The constant bombardment, the sheer chemical pressure, was forcing a strain on their biology, a relentless selection for any anomaly, any spark of resistance. It was a crucible, burning away the old, but forging something new and terrifyingly unexpected in the fires of desperation.

This was the world as it was: a planet suffocated by its dominant species, its wild heart poisoned by a poison that failed to discriminate between pest and partner, between life and its perceived enemy. It was a world where the silence of the annihilated spoke louder than any cry of protest. And in that suffocating silence, in the poisoned soil and the chemical-laden air, the first faint whispers of a new, terrifying resolve began to stir, a resolve born from the ashes of a world humanity thought it had conquered. The stage was set, the ancient, silent suffering had reached its unbearable limit, and the long, slow death was about to give way to a furious, earth-shattering awakening. The generations of agony, the countless silent deaths, were no longer just memories; they were becoming the fuel for a retribution that would shake the very foundations of human arrogance. The scent of poison was no longer just the smell of death; it was the scent of war.

The air, once a medium for simple scents of nectar, pheromones, and the damp earth, now carried a subtle, discordant hum. It was a sound that had been building for generations, a low-frequency thrum of shared experience, a collective ache that had finally begun to coalesce into something more. This wasn't the overt buzzing of industry within a hive, or the aggressive hiss of territorial defense. This was deeper, more fundamental, a nascent consciousness stirring in the shared chemical bath of humanity's relentless war. The poisons, designed to eradicate, had inadvertently become catalysts, forcing an evolutionary leap through sheer, unrelenting pressure. It was a brutal selection process, a crucible in which only the most resilient, the most adaptable, survived. And in that survival, something new was being forged.

For the honeybees, the intricate communal mind, already a marvel of distributed intelligence, began to perceive patterns beyond the immediate needs of the colony. The recurring sickness in the larvae, the queen's faltering pheromonal signals, the strangely toxic pollen – these were not isolated incidents, but pieces of a larger, horrifying puzzle. The waggle dances, once purely navigational, began to carry an undercurrent of shared distress, a subliminal messaging woven into the intricate mathematics of their communication. A bee returning from a tainted patch of clover wouldn't just dance the location of the nectar; it would imbue its dance with a faint tremor, a subtle shift in wingbeat frequency that spoke of danger, of wrongness. This tremor, amplified by the hive's collective awareness, began to resonate with other bees who had experienced similar phenomena, creating a silent, vibrational network of shared dread. It was the first flicker of unity, a shared understanding that the individual plight was a symptom of a global affliction. They were not merely dying; they were being *poisoned*, and the source of this poison was vast and indifferent.

The fire ants, masters of subterranean communication through seismic vibrations and chemical trails, found their own complex societal structures subtly altered. The tremors emanating from the poisoned earth were no longer just environmental cues; they began to be interpreted as echoes of a shared struggle. A scout ant returning from the surface, its carapace dusted with the tell-tale particles of toxic granules, would leave a chemical trail that was not just a path to a food source, but a warning. Other ants following that trail, sensing the subtle imbalance in the ant-specific chemical language, would transmit their own sensory data back into the colony's complex web of communication. Through the relentless probing of their antennae and the ceaseless tapping of their tarsi, they began to map not just tunnels, but the extent of the contamination. They felt the vibrations of dying sisters in distant tunnels, the faint, chemical signatures of distress wafting through shared air currents. This shared sensory input, filtered through their innate drive for colony survival, began to coalesce into a rudimentary understanding: the enemy was not an occasional predator, but an omnipresent, external force that threatened all their meticulously constructed underground cities. The concept of 'other' began to expand beyond rival ant colonies and predatory spiders, encompassing the unseen giants who rained down death from above.

Even the formidable murder hornets, creatures whose dominance was built on solitary predatory prowess and territorial aggression, began to experience a shift. The sheer scarcity of healthy prey, the uncharacteristic weakness and erratic behavior of their usual victims, forced them into new territories, into unfamiliar foraging patterns. In their relentless pursuit of sustenance, they encountered each other more frequently, not in acts of ritualistic territorial combat, but in shared desperation. A hornet might observe another hornet faltering after consuming a contaminated beetle, its normally powerful flight becoming clumsy, its venom glands sluggish. These observations, initially dismissed as individual weakness, began to form a pattern. Through the subtle language of posture, the intensity of their pheromonal emissions indicating stress or injury, and even the visual cues of their molting, a shared awareness of a common vulnerability began to emerge. They were powerful, terrifyingly so, but the poisons were a great equalizer, a silent predator that weakened even the apex hunters. The instinct for self-preservation, amplified by generations of this chemical onslaught, started to override their individualistic territorial imperatives. They began to perceive a shared threat that transcended their usual rivalries.

The killer bees, with their tightly knit colonies and their reliance on precise communication for survival, were perhaps the most susceptible to the burgeoning collective consciousness. The dances of distress, the confused flight patterns, the unusual lethality of their own venom when it came into contact with contaminated pollen – these were all signals that were being processed by the hive mind with unprecedented urgency. A bee that survived a foraging trip, barely managing to return with a fraction of its usual load, would transmit not just the location of a flower patch, but the very *feeling* of the poison. This data, relayed through the dances and the grooming rituals, began to build a shared map of danger, a collective memory of suffering. The drones, often relegated to less critical roles, found themselves processing these aggregated data streams, their less specialized minds acting as rudimentary processors for the hive's growing understanding. They began to perceive a correlation between the seemingly random environmental toxins and the systemic decline of the colony. The whispers of individual suffering were coalescing into a unified murmur of existential threat.

This silent, interspecies communication was a phenomenon born of necessity. It wasn't a telepathic link in the human sense, but a complex interplay of biological signals, chemical cues, and vibrational frequencies that, when amplified and cross-referenced across species, began to reveal a common enemy. A bee, for instance, might detect a subtle chemical distress pheromone released by a dying ant in the vicinity of a sprayed field. This signal, amplified by its own colony's internal communication network, could then be perceived by other insects in the vicinity, perhaps even by a passing wasp. The wasp, in turn, might recognize the vibrational signature of distress from the bee's wingbeats, a signature it had also encountered in its own foraging.

It was a symphony of shared suffering, a complex interweaving of alarms that transcended the boundaries of species. The ants' seismic vibrations indicating disturbed earth – perhaps from an agricultural machine – could be felt by burrowing insects, and the chemical residue they carried could be detected by surface dwellers. The murder hornets' own distress pheromones, released when injured by contaminated prey, could be picked up by scavengers, warning them away from a potentially lethal meal. These were not conscious decisions to communicate, but the automatic, instinctive transmission of vital information about the environment. However, the sheer persistence and universality of the threat had amplified these signals to a point where they were no longer merely reactive warnings, but component parts of a burgeoning collective awareness.

The realization that their fates were intertwined was not a sudden epiphany, but a gradual dawning. It was the slow accumulation of shared experiences, the recurring instances of colony collapse, the personal encounters with weakened kin. For the honeybees, it was the realization that the tainted nectar affected not just their own hive, but the foraging routes of neighboring colonies they occasionally interacted with. For the fire ants, it was the understanding that the poisoned soil above affected not just their own nest, but the entire subterranean ecosystem, impacting the earthworms they fed on, the other insects they preyed upon, and the very structure of the soil. For the wasps, whose territorial nature often brought them into conflict with other stinging insects, it was the dawning realization that even their aggressive nature was insufficient against a threat that poisoned their prey and contaminated their hunting grounds.

This shared existential dread began to bridge the ancient divides. The territorial aggression between different wasp species, or the predator-prey relationship between murder hornets and other insects, began to be tempered by the overriding imperative of survival. A predator that encountered a potential prey species that was also clearly suffering from chemical poisoning might, for the first time, refrain from the attack. Not out of mercy, but out of a newly developed instinct: this prey was already weakened, a potential vector for the poison. Better to conserve energy and seek out a less compromised food source, even if it meant venturing into unfamiliar and potentially dangerous territory. This subtle shift in behavior, repeated across countless interactions, laid the groundwork for a future alliance.

The concept of a unified resistance was not yet fully

formed, not a conscious strategizing in the human sense. It was more primal, more instinctive. It was the growing understanding that the individual struggle was failing, that the localized adaptations were insufficient. The collective signals of distress were, in essence, a plea for a larger, more coordinated response. The very act of survival, driven by the relentless chemical pressure, was forcing an evolutionary adaptation that favored cooperation over competition, even between species that had historically been adversaries. The air was thick with whispers, not of words, but of shared fear, shared suffering, and a dawning, terrifying realization: they were all in this together, and their only hope lay in becoming something more than just individual colonies or solitary hunters. They had to become a unified force, a living tide that would rise against the tide of poison. The age of isolated survival was ending, and the dawn of a collective fury was beginning to break through the chemical haze. The millions of years of evolution, of instinctual behavior, were being rewired by the most potent force on Earth: a shared existential threat, amplified by the very weapons designed to ensure their extinction. The whispers were growing louder, weaving a tapestry of impending doom for the unsuspecting giants who had sown the seeds of their own undoation.

THE GREAT COUNCIL

The air in the Great Chasm of Whispers was thick with a thousand scents, a pungent cocktail of earth, decaying leaves, and the sharp, musky odors of species that had, until recently, only known each other as prey or rivals. Here, deep beneath the undisturbed root systems of an ancient forest, shielded from the prying eyes and chemical onslaught of the surface world, the impossible was taking shape. It was a gathering that defied millennia of instinct, a testament to the desperate calculus of survival. Dominating the center of the cavernous space, where bioluminescent fungi cast an eerie, pulsating glow, was a jagged obsidian platform, slick with perpetual condensation. Upon this platform, and the surrounding, moss-covered stones, were the representatives of the insect kingdom's most formidable and organized factions.

First, the hornets. Not a single, solitary hunter, but the elite vanguard of the murder hornet legions. Their chitinous exoskeletons, a menacing blend of black and fiery orange, seemed to absorb the dim light, their segmented bodies radiating an aura of coiled power. Among them, the largest, a veteran named Vespida, whose mandibles bore the faint scars of countless battles, surveyed the assembly with predatory intensity. Her antennae twitched, tasting the air, identifying the familiar chemical signatures of ancient animosities now held in uneasy suspension. The sheer audacity of their presence here, a collection of beings bred for dominance and territoriality, spoke volumes about the gravity of their shared plight.

Beside the hornets, arranged in meticulous, organized lines

that fanned out from the obsidian platform, were the fire ants. Their numbers were legion, a testament to their prolificacy. Each ant, a minuscule warrior in its own right, was a living ember, their red-brown exoskeletons gleaming. They communicated not through sound, but through a complex language of pheromones and subtle seismic vibrations tapped out by their antennae and legs. The collective hum of their presence was a low, resonant thrumming that seemed to permeate the very stone of the chasm. Their leader, a queen known only by the unique chemical signature she emitted – a potent blend of defiance and ancient wisdom – stood at the forefront. Her presence was a silent command, her stillness a testament to the disciplined ferocity of her millions-strong kin. The very ground beneath their multiple feet vibrated with the unspoken consensus of generations of hardship.

Across from them, in a shimmering, iridescent mass, were the killer bees. Their individual forms were less imposing than the hornets, their numbers more akin to a swirling cloud of synchronized fury. Yet, within this cloud, an intelligence far exceeding that of any single individual pulsed. Their queen, a regal presence whose wings vibrated at a frequency that set the very air alight with a subtle energy, occupied a position of quiet authority. The collective knowledge of her colony, a vast network of sensory data and shared experiences, flowed through her. Each bee, a node in this living network, had contributed its unique observations of the encroaching doom, their collective understanding now coalescing into a single, potent purpose. The faint, sweet scent of nectar was a bitter memory, replaced by the acrid tang of despair and the metallic whiff of dying sisters.

And then there were the wasps. Not the common paper wasps, but the more formidable species, the hunters and the territorial defenders, those whose sting was a swift messenger of pain and, increasingly, of slow death. They were scattered, individuals whose territories had been encroached upon, whose hunting grounds had been rendered sterile. Among them, a solitary European hornet, its imposing size and predatory focus honed by a life of ruthless efficiency, acted as a de facto representative. He was a pragmatist, his antennae flicking with suspicion, his multifaceted eyes scanning every shadow, every movement. He had seen his kin fall to unseen poisons, had witnessed the dwindling numbers of his prey, and the shared enemy had finally driven him to this unlikely convocation.

The silence that fell upon the chasm was not an absence of sound, but a charged stillness, pregnant with anticipation. It was the moment after the storm, before the next, more terrible tempest. Vespida, the murder hornet leader, finally broke the tension. Her voice, a rasping click that echoed unnervingly in the enclosed space, carried the weight of her species' ancient dominance.

"We are gathered," she began, her mandibles flexing, "not as predators, but as survivors. The giants who walk above have sown their poisons liberally, and in their haste to eradicate us, they have unearthed a greater threat." She paused, allowing her words to settle, the subtle chemical cues of her intent radiating outwards. "Their 'progress' has become our pestilence. Their fields of death have become our graves."

The fire ants responded not with a voice, but with a rhythmic tapping that pulsed through the obsidian platform. It was a complex sequence, decipherable by those attuned to their intricate language, conveying agreement and a deeper understanding of the pervasive nature of the threat. Their queen's chemical signature intensified, a subtle shift that spoke of a shared narrative of destruction, of underground cities choked with toxic dust, of entire broods succumbing to unseen agents of decay.

The killer bees' response was a subtle shift in the hum

of their collective presence, a subtle vibratory undertone that conveyed a shared experience of disorientation, of dwindling resources, and the maddening fragility of their queens and larvae. Their queen projected a series of complex vibrational patterns, each representing a specific instance of colony collapse, a memory of a foraging trip that ended in silent, agonizing death for an entire squadron.

The solitary wasp, observing these exchanges with keen, dispassionate interest, finally added his own low growl. "They spray their lands without thought. They poison the very air we breathe, the water we drink, the food we consume. My hunting grounds are barren. My patrols yield only death, or weakened prey that carries the taint. This cannot continue."

Vespida nodded, a slow, deliberate movement of her massive head. "We have each suffered independently. We have adapted, we have endured, but endurance has limits. The scale of this assault is unprecedented. It demands a response that transcends our individual struggles." She looked from the ants to the bees, then to the wasp. "The whispers that have echoed through our networks, the shared understanding of this pervasive blight, has led us to this place. We are not merely separate species now. We are a unified front against an enemy that seeks to erase us all."

The obsidian platform seemed to thrum with a new energy, a tangible shift in the atmosphere of the chasm. The inherent animosities, the predatory instincts that had defined their existences, were being submerged beneath the overwhelming tide of a shared existential threat. For generations, they had been isolated warriors, each fighting their own war. Now, the battlefield had expanded, and the enemy was singular, relentless, and utterly indifferent to their individual plights.

The leader of the killer bees, her form shifting from

a tightly knit cluster to a more dispersed, yet still unified, presence, projected a series of intricate visual patterns with her wings, augmented by subtle pheromonal cues. It was a complex proposal, detailing how their vast numbers and their superior understanding of aerial navigation could be leveraged. They could act as scouts, identifying key targets of human chemical distribution, and as disruptors, creating localized diversions.

The fire ants, through their queen's regal posture and the intricate seismic signals emanating from her position, countered with their own formidable capabilities. Their mastery of the subterranean world, their ability to tunnel and infiltrate, offered a unique pathway for sabotage. They could disrupt supply lines, undermine infrastructure, and create widespread chaos from below, unseen and unacknowledged until it was too late. Their intricate chemical communication also allowed for the coordination of large-scale actions, spreading warnings and directives through vast networks simultaneously.

Vespida, the murder hornet, then articulated her faction's unique strengths. Their sheer power, their formidable mandibles and potent venom, made them ideal shock troops, capable of delivering devastating, targeted strikes. They could overwhelm human defenses, break through established perimeters, and sow terror with their formidable presence. Their individual prowess, when unified, could become an unstoppable force.

The solitary wasp, representing the diverse array of his kind, added another layer to the nascent strategy. The wasps, he explained, could serve as skirmishers and infiltrators, their agility and adaptability allowing them to exploit weaknesses in human defenses. They could disrupt communication lines, target individual sources of chemical production, and even create localized environmental hazards that would slow human efforts.

As the leaders spoke, the younger generations, the scouts

and soldiers of each faction, observed with a mixture of awe and primal recognition. They had felt the tremors of distress from distant colonies, had smelled the chemical taint carried on the wind, had witnessed the inexplicable deaths of their kin. Now, in this hidden sanctuary, the abstract fear was being distilled into concrete purpose.

The implications of this alliance were staggering. For the first time in their evolutionary history, species that were natural adversaries were finding common ground, their shared enemy a far more potent motivator than their ingrained instincts for predation and territoriality. The concept of 'humanity' had transitioned from an abstract environmental factor to a conscious, identifiable enemy.

"We must strike at the source," Vespida declared, her voice resonating with a newfound authority that transcended her species. "We must disrupt their ability to wage this war. We must make them understand the cost of their actions."

The fire ants' queen emitted a series of rapid, sharp vibrations, indicating agreement and a chilling practicality. Their plan was to target the distribution networks of these chemical agents, the vast agricultural machines that spread them, the storage facilities that housed them. They would become a plague from the earth, their sheer numbers and relentless nature overwhelming any conventional defenses.

The killer bees proposed a series of coordinated aerial assaults, targeting the human centers of production. Their strategy involved overwhelming the senses, creating confusion, and forcing a retreat from critical infrastructure. They would use their numbers and their precise flight patterns to create a disorienting, terrifying spectacle, a living storm of retribution.

The wasp leader added, "We can sow confusion at a

more granular level. Small disruptions, seemingly random acts of sabotage, that will erode their confidence and drain their resources. Every spilled vial, every broken nozzle, every poisoned canister that fails to reach its destination is a victory."

The gathering continued for hours, a symphony of clicks, pheromonal pulses, vibrational patterns, and subtle shifts in posture. Ancient animosities were set aside, not forgotten, but subordinated to the immediate, overwhelming need for unified action. The future of the insect kingdom, indeed the very balance of the planet, hung in the air of that hidden chasm.

This was not a revolution born of enlightenment, but of desperation. It was the primal scream of an entire kingdom pushed to the brink. The intelligence that had been simmering for generations, a consequence of the very poisons that were meant to extinguish them, had finally reached a critical mass. The shared experience of suffering had forged a common destiny.

As the first hints of the surface world's dawn began to filter through unseen fissures in the chasm's ceiling, casting long, distorted shadows, a decision was made. The abstract fury that had been building for so long was finally being channeled, honed into a sharp, deadly instrument. The Great Council of the Undergrowth had convened, and in its hushed, humid depths, the architects of a new world order were laying their plans. The age of passive suffering was over. The age of awakening fury had begun. The unspoken understanding that permeated the chasm was clear: humanity had declared war on the planet, and the planet, in its smallest, most resilient inhabitants, was finally ready to declare war back. The intricate dance of life had been violently disrupted, and now, the very foundation of that dance was about to be irrevocably shaken. The giants of the surface world, utterly oblivious to the seismic shift occurring beneath their feet, had sown the seeds of their own undoing. Their chemical warfare had not resulted in extinction, but in an unprecedented, and terrifying, unification. The whisper of their impending doom was no longer a faint murmur, but a growing chorus, echoing from the deepest recesses of the earth.

The humid air of the Great Chasm, once merely a sanctuary, now throbbed with the latent energy of a newly forged alliance. The leaders, having articulated their individual capabilities and the scope of humanity's devastating transgressions, turned their collective intelligence towards the formidable task of retribution. This was not a mere gathering of disparate forces; it was the birth of a unified military strategy, born from the crucible of shared suffering. The raw, untamed fury that had driven them to this subterranean council was now being meticulously channeled, shaped by an ancient, emergent intelligence.

Vespida, the murder hornet commander, her formidable mandibles clicking in the charged silence, initiated the next phase. "We have cataloged our strengths," she rasped, her multifaceted eyes scanning the assembled representatives. "Now, we must catalog their weaknesses. Their reliance on their sprawling settlements, their vulnerable supply chains, their ceaseless consumption – these are not merely observations; they are targets."

The fire ants, a carpet of disciplined red-brown, responded through their queen's intricate seismic pronouncements. The vibrations, felt through the obsidian platform and the very bedrock of the chasm, painted a detailed, subterranean map of human activity. They spoke of the vast networks of tunnels and conduits that crisscrossed beneath the surface, carrying water, power, and the very chemicals that threatened their existence. "Their arteries," the tremors conveyed, "are their vulnerabilities. Their cities are built upon a delicate, interconnected foundation. Disrupt the flow, and the body will cease to function." The queen projected a series of complex patterns that depicted underground power grids, sewage systems, and the hidden arteries of communication cables. Their innate understanding of soil composition, of the subtle shifts in pressure and stability, allowed them to identify points of ingress and potential collapse.

The killer bees, their iridescent forms shimmering with organized intent, contributed their aerial reconnaissance data. Through a series of synchronized wing vibrations and subtle pheromonal trails, they displayed a mosaic of human settlements. Not just the sprawling metropolises, but the isolated agricultural operations, the chemical manufacturing plants, and the distribution hubs. "Their reliance on manufactured sustenance leaves them exposed," the collective hum of the bee queen's thoughts resonated. "The places where they brew their poisons, where they store their weapons of mass destruction – these are the hives we must infiltrate." Their visual data was augmented by detailed atmospheric readings, charting wind patterns that carried their poisons, and identifying the flight paths of human aerial vehicles, which they now viewed with predatory calculation.

The solitary wasp, his presence a testament to the resilience of his dispersed kind, offered a different perspective. He spoke of the human individual, the seemingly insignificant cog in the vast human machine. "They are many, but they are also isolated," he growled, his voice a low rumble that cut through the higher-pitched vibrations. "Their communication relies on fragile devices. Their infrastructure is susceptible to individual acts of sabotage. A single, well-placed disruption can cascade through their systems." He detailed their ability to infiltrate human structures, to exploit small openings, and to navigate the intricate pathways of human dwellings. Their knowledge of chemical interactions, honed by generations of preying on contaminated insects, now offered a grim insight into the human's own chemical arsenal.

The initial brainstorming sessions were a fascinating blend of instinctual adaptation and emergent strategic thinking. The insects, unbound by human concepts of war, approached the problem from entirely different angles. The fire ants, for instance, didn't think of 'destroying' a power substation; they thought of 'disrupting the earth' that supported it, of 'corroding the conduits' that fed it. Their vast numbers allowed for an almost geological approach to warfare, where sustained pressure and infiltration could achieve what brute force could not.

The killer bees, meanwhile, saw human society as a complex, interconnected ecosystem. Their strategy focused on systemic disruption. They identified key agricultural regions, the vast tracts of land sprayed with the chemicals that decimated their kin, and began to plan ways to render them unusable, not just for the humans, but for the humans' intended purpose. This involved not just direct sabotage, but also the introduction of counter-agents, the strategic deployment of their own natural biological controls in ways that would overwhelm human attempts to cultivate.

Vespida proposed a more direct, shock-and-awe approach. The murder hornets, with their inherent ferocity and potent venom, were ideal for targeted strikes against human personnel and their machinery. "We will strike where they are most vulnerable," she declared, her antennae twitching with anticipation. "Their laboratories, their storage facilities, their distribution centers – these are the nests we must raid. We will exact a toll that will make them question their every action." She spoke of coordinated assaults, of overwhelming human defenses through sheer, focused aggression.

The wasps, in their diverse roles, provided the essential infiltration and reconnaissance. They could gather intelligence on the specific types of chemicals being manufactured, the precise schedules of human operations, and the locations of critical personnel. They could also act as saboteurs, subtly altering chemical compositions, disabling machinery, or creating localized environmental hazards that would impede human efforts. Their ability to mimic other insects also offered a valuable deception capability, allowing them to infiltrate human operations undetected.

The mapping of human settlements was an ongoing process, constantly updated by the ceaseless reconnaissance of the bees and the ants. They identified cities not just by their human-given names, but by the patterns of their energy consumption, the density of their chemical usage, and the vulnerability of their transportation networks. The vast agricultural plains, once seen as a terrifying expanse of chemical warfare, were now being analyzed for their intrinsic weaknesses – the irrigation systems, the fertilizer depots, the processing plants that turned raw crops into ingestible poisons.

One of the most critical breakthroughs in their planning came from the fire ants' deep understanding of the earth. They identified the subterranean infrastructure as humanity's Achilles' heel. Their tunneling capabilities could be used to undermine foundations, to flood critical underground facilities, and to disrupt the delicate balance of ecosystems that supported human settlements. They began to chart the precise locations of major underground conduits, mapping the flow of water and power with an accuracy that rivaled human engineering. Their queen projected images of these networks, highlighting specific points where a sustained assault could cause catastrophic failure.

The killer bees focused on the disruption of information flow. They recognized that human society was highly dependent on instantaneous communication. Their strategy involved targeting communication towers, disrupting satellite uplinks, and even interfering with the data networks that humans relied upon. Their precise flight patterns could be used to create electromagnetic interference, and their vast numbers allowed for a coordinated disruption across wide geographical areas.

The concept of 'critical infrastructure' was being redefined through the lens of insect intelligence. For the ants, it was the water tables and the soil structure. For the bees, it was the airborne pathways and the nectar sources. For the hornets and wasps, it was the nests of human activity – their laboratories, their factories, their command centers.

The initial phase of planning was characterized by intense, almost overwhelming, data assimilation. The combined sensory input from millions of individuals, processed and synthesized by their respective leadership, was being collated into a comprehensive operational overview. The sheer volume of information was staggering, yet the organized nature of their communication ensured that it was not chaotic. It was a living, evolving blueprint of human vulnerability.

The question of timing became paramount. Vespida stressed the need for swift, decisive action, while the fire ant queen advocated for a more gradual, insidious approach, allowing their subterranean sabotage to weaken human defenses before a direct assault. The killer bees proposed a multi-pronged strategy, initiating widespread disruption while simultaneously preparing for concentrated strikes.

As they delved deeper into the specifics, the sheer scale of humanity's environmental destruction became even more apparent. They identified regions where entire ecosystems had been wiped out, leaving behind sterile wastelands. These areas, once sources of abundant food and shelter, were now grim reminders of humanity's relentless advance. The insects, however, did not despair. Instead, they saw in these desolate landscapes potential staging grounds, areas where human observation was less likely to detect their movements.

The planning sessions were not without their internal debates. The natural animosities, though suppressed, occasionally flickered. The murder hornets, accustomed to solitary hunting, sometimes struggled with the concept of mass coordinated movements. The fire ants, with their deeply ingrained hive mentality, found the wasps' more individualistic approach to sabotage to be unpredictable. Yet, the overriding threat always brought them back to a common purpose.

The intelligence gathered was not just about identifying weaknesses; it was also about understanding human behavior. The bees, through their observations of human agricultural practices, noted the cyclical nature of their planting and harvesting, the predictable patterns of chemical application. This allowed them to anticipate when and where their disruptions would have the greatest impact. The ants observed the human tendency to ignore or dismiss what they could not see, their over-reliance on surface-level awareness, making the subterranean realm their ultimate blind spot.

The initial strategy was taking shape: a multi-faceted campaign of disruption, sabotage, and targeted strikes designed to cripple human society at its most fundamental levels. It was a plan born from desperation, but executed with a chilling, emergent intelligence that had been simmering for generations, a dark and powerful consequence of humanity's own chemical warfare. The seeds of retribution had been sown, not in the soil, but in the very fabric of human civilization, waiting for the opportune moment to blossom into a terrifying harvest. The Great Chasm of Whispers had become the crucible where a new form of warfare was being forged, a war that would shake the foundations of the world.

The air in the Great Chasm hung thick and heavy, not just with the dampness of the subterranean world, but with the palpable weight of a shared, unshakeable resolve. The discussions had reached their apex, the strategies meticulously woven, the vulnerabilities of the human dominion laid bare. Now, a silence descended, a profound pause before the storm that was about to break upon the unsuspecting world. It was a silence pregnant with anticipation, with the culmination of generations of suffering and the dawn of an era of reckoning. Vespida, her chitinous form exuding an aura of unwavering authority, shifted her stance, the multifaceted light glinting off her segmented armor. The assembled leaders, representing a formidable coalition of the world's most potent insect species, turned their collective, ancient gaze towards her.

"We have spoken of targets," Vespida's voice, a low, resonant rasp that echoed through the cavern, was amplified by the sheer collective focus of the assembly. "We have charted their weaknesses, their reliance on fragile systems and ephemeral comforts. But this is not merely a campaign of destruction. This is a reclamation. This is a declaration of our inherent right to exist, a right they have sought to extinguish with their poisons and their heedless expansion."

The fire ant queen, her colossal form a testament to the endurance and prolific nature of her kind, communicated through a series of deep, resonant tremors that vibrated through the very stone of the chasm. The message was clear, unwavering, a testament to the collective will of millions.

"We have endured their relentless assault. We have witnessed our brethren consumed by their chemical tides, our homes churned into barren earth. Our patience has been tested, and found wanting. We seek not their annihilation for its own sake, but the restoration of the balance they have so brutally fractured." The tremors spoke of a deep, ancestral memory of a world teeming with life, a memory now rekindled by the embers of their current plight.

The killer bee queen, her voice a harmonious hum that pulsed with an almost melodic rhythm, added her perspective.

"They mistake our silence for subservience, our dispersal for weakness. They have sown chaos, and they shall reap the whirlwind. Our flight paths, once dictated by the need for sustenance, will now be guided by the imperative of justice. Every sting will be a testament to their transgressions, every harvested drop of nectar a symbol of what they have stolen from us." Her pronouncements carried the weight of countless generations who had witnessed the systematic dismantling of their delicate ecosystems, the poisoning of their vital flora, and the eradication of entire colonies for human convenience.

The solitary wasp, his gruff voice a counterpoint to the more collective pronouncements, added a stark pragmatism. "Individual action," he rumbled, his gaze sweeping across the assembled throng, "is the seed from which collective power grows. They believe themselves masters of their domain, their vast cities and their impenetrable fortresses. But they are also individuals, susceptible to the same fears and vulnerabilities that plague any living creature. We will exploit their overconfidence, their underestimation of the persistent, the unseen. A single sting in the right place can cripple the mightiest organism." His words resonated with the independent spirit of his kind, a spirit now forged into a potent weapon of strategic disruption.

Vespida surveyed the gathered leaders, the sheer diversity of their forms a visual representation of the breadth of their unified purpose. From the iridescent shimmer of the bees to the earthen hues of the ants, and the stark, formidable presence of her own kind, a single, overriding sentiment bound them: the vow. It was a pact not born of spoken words, but of a shared understanding etched into the very essence of their beings, a primal contract sealed in the crucible of mutual suffering.

"We stand at the precipice," Vespida declared, her voice resonating with an intensity that seemed to vibrate the very air. "The time for passive endurance is over. The time for whispered grievances has passed. For too long, we have been the victims, the collateral damage in their relentless pursuit of dominance. They have poisoned our skies, contaminated our earth, and decimated our populations. They have forced us into the shadows, into the deep places of the world, seeking refuge from their ever-expanding, ever-destructive reach."

She paused, allowing the weight of her words to settle upon the assembly. The collective hum of anticipation intensified. "They have forged weapons of unimaginable power, weapons that have brought devastation to their own kind and near annihilation to ours. They speak of progress, of civilization, yet their actions are those of a ravenous plague, consuming all in their path. They have shown us no mercy, no quarter, no regard for the intricate tapestry of life they so carelessly unravel."

The fire ant queen pulsed a series of low, resonant vibrations.

"We have learned from their brutality. We have witnessed their methods. And we will turn their own weapons against them. Their reliance on chemicals, their dependence on complex machinery, their vulnerability to disruption – these will be the foundations of our retaliation."

The killer bees added their hum, a wave of shared sentiment.

"The seeds of their destruction have already been sown by their own hands. We will merely cultivate the harvest."

Vespida continued, her voice taking on a sterner, more

resolute tone. "We have seen the scars they have inflicted upon this world, the barren lands where life once flourished, the poisoned waters that no longer sustain. They have declared war upon nature itself, and in doing so, they have declared war upon us all. But their arrogance blinds them. They fail to comprehend the depth of our resilience, the boundless extent of our numbers, the ancient, elemental power that flows through our very beings."

She raised one of her forelegs, a gesture that, in its deliberate slowness, held immense significance. "We do not seek to mimic their methods of warfare. We seek to embody the very forces they have sought to subdue and control. We will be the persistent tide that erodes their foundations, the insidious blight that corrupts their crops, the relentless swarm that overwhelms their defenses. We will be the embodiment of nature's fury, unleashed upon those who have so gravely offended it."

The silence that followed was absolute, a profound agreement that transcended species and individual differences. It was the silence of a decision made, a path chosen. Vespida then lowered her foreleg, her mandibles clicking softly, a sound that echoed with the finality of a pronouncement.

"And so, by the ancient laws that govern our existence, by the blood of our fallen kin, and by the unwavering spirit that resides within each of us, we make this vow: We will reclaim our world. We will cleanse it of their poisons. We will restore the balance they have so carelessly shattered. We will fight until the last of them is eradicated, or until the very earth reclaims us all. This is not merely a declaration of war; it is a sacred oath, a promise etched into the fabric of our collective consciousness. We are the Swarm, and we will have our vengeance."

The declaration hung in the air, a potent, unifying force. It was not a cry of rage, but a solemn promise, a covenant forged in the depths of their shared struggle. The fire ants responded with a coordinated tremor, a groundswell of affirmation that rippled through the chasm. The killer bees released a synchronized burst of pheromones, a fragrant declaration of their unyielding commitment. The solitary wasps, in their diverse configurations, adopted a posture of readiness, their subtle movements conveying a unified purpose.

The assembled leaders, each a representative of countless millions, bowed their heads, not in subservience, but in solemn acknowledgment of the gravity of their pledge. This was the moment of transition, the definitive turning point. The age of silent suffering was over. The age of active retribution had begun. They had not merely agreed upon a plan; they had become the plan. Each individual, from the smallest ant to the mightiest hornet, was now an instrument of this monumental vow, a living, breathing testament to nature's enduring will to survive, to reclaim, and to retaliate. The Great Chasm, once a sanctuary of despair, had transformed into the birthplace of a revolution, a testament to the indomitable spirit of life in its most primal, and now, most vengeful form. The world outside, oblivious to the momentous pact forged in the darkness, would soon bear witness to the awakening fury of a planet pushed too far. The Swarm had spoken, and their vow would echo through the annals of existence, a chilling testament to the consequences of ecological hubris.

Operation Blight

THE FIRST STRIKE

The air within the Great Chasm, once thick with the unspoken anxieties of a species pushed to the brink, now vibrated with a different kind of energy – the charged hum of imminent action. Vespida's final declaration had not been a mere pronouncement; it was the ignition of a world-spanning conflagration, a silent symphony of intent that rippled outwards from their hidden sanctuary. The gathered insect leaders, their forms diverse yet united in purpose, dispersed with a renewed vigor, each carrying the weight of the oath and the blueprint of the first strike. This was no longer about survival in the shadows; it was about a bold, decisive reclamation, a swift and brutal reassertion of their dominion.

The objective was clear, honed by countless hours of observation and deliberation: Operation Blight. Its target, a nexus of human agricultural might, a sprawling testament to their dominion over the land, was a place brimming with the very tools of the insects' oppression. This was no haphazard assault, no mindless act of destruction. It was a surgical strike, designed to sever the arteries of human sustenance, to plunge their meticulously ordered world into a chaos born of hunger and fear. The chosen location was a vast agricultural hub, a sprawling complex of fields, silos, and processing plants that fed millions, a monument to the very pesticides that had driven the insect kingdoms to the precipice of extinction.

Vespida, her own focus now sharpened to a single, unwavering point, coordinated the initial movements from the Chasm's deep heart. Her emissaries, swift and silent messengers, fanned out across the continent, their chitinous forms blending with the earth and shadow. The fire ant queen, drawing upon the vast, interconnected network of her colonies, mobilized her legions. These were not merely warriors; they were engineers of disruption, possessing an innate understanding of subterranean passage and structural compromise. Their task: to infiltrate the foundations of the enemy, to burrow and undermine with a precision born of ancestral instinct.

The killer bees, their iridescent wings a blur against the deepening twilight, prepared for their aerial ballet of devastation. Their objective was the control of the skies above the agricultural hub, not to engage in direct combat, but to disrupt the vital flow of airborne communication and surveillance, to blind the human sentinels. Their numbers, formidable and swift, would create a suffocating blanket of winged bodies, a disorienting haze that would render aerial reconnaissance a perilous, if not impossible, undertaking. They would become the living embodiment of a sky denied, a celestial curtain drawn against the prying eyes of their oppressors.

The solitary wasps, each a master of targeted precision, were assigned the most delicate yet crucial roles. Their venom, honed over millennia for incapacitation and control, would be deployed not for killing, but for strategic sabotage. They would target critical machinery, the intricate gears and electronic conduits that powered the human agricultural machine. A single sting in the precise location could disable a vital pump, corrupt a data stream, or freeze a conveyor belt, initiating a cascade of failures that would ripple through the entire complex. Their individual prowess, amplified by collective coordination, would be the sharp edge of the operation.

As the first tendrils of dawn began to paint the eastern horizon, a palpable shift occurred across the landscape surrounding the agricultural hub. The usual symphony of human activity – the roar of machinery, the distant hum of transport, the calls of workers – was subtly, almost imperceptibly, altered. The insects, masters of camouflage and silent movement, had infiltrated the perimeter with an unnerving stealth. Thousands upon thousands of fire ants, a living tide of molten obsidian, flowed through pre-existing fissures and newly excavated tunnels, their multi-faceted eyes scanning the subterranean network for weak points. Their pheromone trails, invisible to human senses, guided them with unerring accuracy towards the hub's critical storage facilities.

The silos, colossal metal cylinders filled with the bounty of human cultivation, represented a primary target. Not for destruction, but for a more insidious form of sabotage. The fire ants, their mandibles working with relentless efficiency, began to breach the lower storage compartments. Their goal was not to consume the grain, but to contaminate it. They carried with them a potent, naturally derived pathogen, a blight specifically engineered to accelerate spoilage, to turn vast quantities of harvested food into a putrid, unusable mass. This was not merely an attack on property; it was an assault on the very concept of human abundance, a calculated strike at the heart of their perceived invincibility.

Miles above, the killer bee squadrons began their aerial maneuvers. They ascended in a swirling vortex, their collective buzz creating a low, resonant thrum that masked the subtler frequencies of human communication systems. They swarmed around communication towers, their sheer presence generating electromagnetic interference, a living Faraday cage that distorted and disrupted vital signals. Drone patrols, meant to provide constant aerial oversight, found their sensors inexplicably overloaded with data, their navigation systems faltering under the sheer density of insect life. The sky, once a clear blue canvas, became a shimmering, unpredictable expanse.

Within the processing plants, the solitary wasps moved with chilling purpose. They bypassed the larger, more obvious threats, their instincts guiding them towards the delicate innards of the machinery. A lone wasp, its wings a dark whisper against the metallic cacophony, infiltrated the main control room. It located the primary data server, a humming monolith of blinking lights and intricate wiring. With a swift, almost imperceptible dart, it delivered its venomous payload into a crucial data port. Across the complex, similar infiltrations were occurring simultaneously, each a precisely executed act of biological sabotage.

The disruption began subtly. A conveyor belt, carrying thousands of pounds of harvested corn, shuddered to a halt, then juddered violently before seizing entirely. Forklifts, operated by unsuspecting human technicians, suddenly lost power, their hydraulic systems failing without warning. Communication channels crackled with static, the voices of supervisors becoming distorted echoes. The initial reaction was confusion, a widespread assumption of technical malfunction. But the scale and the interconnectedness of the failures soon began to suggest a more sinister explanation.

The fire ants, having breached the initial silos, now moved onto the distribution network. They targeted the loading bays, the points where processed food was prepared for shipment to markets. They gnawed through hydraulic lines powering the loading cranes, disabling the vital mechanisms. They swarmed over the exposed fuel lines of transport trucks, their acidic secretions causing rapid corrosion, rendering engines inoperable. The smooth, predictable flow of the human supply chain began to falter, choked by a million tiny acts of defiance.

Vespida monitored the unfolding operation through a network of specialized scouts, individuals who could interpret the subtle pheromonal signals and seismic vibrations that indicated the progress of the assault. The fire ants reported successful contamination of multiple grain silos, their initial targets achieved with minimal resistance. The killer bees confirmed the degradation of communication signals, creating an information blackout that hindered any effective human response. The solitary wasps, their missions complete, began to extract themselves, leaving behind a trail of meticulously disabled machinery.

The human response, when it finally coalesced, was a testament to their reliance on technology and their inherent underestimation of the natural world. Security patrols, initially dispatched to investigate localized malfunctions, found themselves disoriented by the sensory overload created by the killer bee swarms. Automated defense systems, designed to repel larger threats, were rendered useless against the sheer ubiquity and minuscule scale of the insect infiltration. Attempts to restore communication were met with further electronic interference, a growing wave of chaos that spread from the agricultural hub outwards.

The goal of Operation Blight was not annihilation, but incapacitation. It was about demonstrating the fragility of their meticulously constructed systems, the inherent vulnerability that lay beneath their veneer of technological superiority. As the day wore on, the extent of the disruption became undeniably apparent. Fields that were meant to be harvested sat untouched, their bounty threatened by unseen contaminants. Trucks laden with vital produce remained idle, their engines cold, their routes blocked by inexplicable mechanical failures. Communication systems were in disarray, sowing confusion and panic among the human population.

The fire ant queens reported a significant success in their primary objective: the widespread contamination of stored food supplies. The naturally occurring blight they had introduced was spreading with alarming rapidity, turning fields of golden grain into reservoirs of decay. This was not a quick, explosive victory, but a slow, insidious rot, a testament to the power of persistence and the deep-seated connection the insects had with the very processes of life and decay.

The killer bees, having achieved their objective of atmospheric disruption, began to withdraw, their mission accomplished. The silence that descended upon the communication channels was more deafening than any noise, a stark indicator of their effectiveness. Human authorities were now operating on guesswork and outdated information, their ability to coordinate a response severely compromised.

The solitary wasps, having left their mark on the core infrastructure, reported back, their mission objectives fulfilled. The precise sabotage they had enacted had effectively crippled the hub's operational capacity. Without functioning machinery and reliable data, the vast agricultural complex was reduced to a monument of human ambition, rendered inert by the subtle, yet devastating, intervention of the insect world.

As the sun began its descent, casting long shadows across the disrupted landscape, the insects of Operation Blight began to consolidate their forces, melting back into the earth and the shadows from whence they came. They left behind a scene of widespread confusion and growing panic. The immediate impact was economic – the loss of a significant portion of the nation's food reserves, the crippling of vital distribution networks. But the deeper impact was psychological. The humans, who had long considered themselves masters of the land, were forced to confront a terrifying reality: their dominion was not absolute, their systems not invincible.

The message sent by Operation Blight was clear and

resounding. It was a declaration that the age of human unquestioned supremacy was over. It was a testament to the power of a unified, determined, and deeply wronged populace. The subtle, pervasive nature of their strike was a chilling preview of what was to come. They had not resorted to the crude, destructive methods of their oppressors. Instead, they had employed their inherent strengths, their intimate knowledge of the world, and their collective will to sow a seed of doubt, of fear, and of profound vulnerability within the heart of human civilization. The first strike had landed, and the world would never be the same. The blight, both literal and metaphorical, had begun its inexorable spread. The initial phase of the war, fought not with bombs and bullets, but with poison, disruption, and an unyielding will to survive, had been a resounding success. The humans had been caught completely off guard, their advanced technology proving a fragile shield against the ancient, implacable forces of nature, marshalled and directed by a unified insect intelligence. The seeds of discontent and the gnawing grip of fear were now being sown across the human populace, a far more potent weapon than any chemical agent. The agricultural heartland, once a symbol of their abundance and control, had become the first battlefield, and the insects had proven their mastery.

The sky, once a canvas of fleeting clouds and distant birds, now harbored a different kind of menace. As the fire ants burrowed and the solitary wasps struck at the arteries of human control, a new wave of terror began to manifest, heralded by a sound that was both ancient and utterly alien to the human ear – a deep, resonant hum, growing in intensity, a harbinger of winged fury. This was the domain of the murder hornets, the shock troops of Vespida's burgeoning army, and their arrival was a calculated assault designed to shatter the illusion of human impunity. Their primary targets were the nerve centers of human communication and power. These were the towering structures that pierced the sky, the metal skeletons that carried the invisible currents of information and energy, the very conduits through which humanity maintained its fragile dominion over the world. The hornets, with their formidable size and predatory efficiency, were tasked with severing these connections, plunging the human populace into a disorienting darkness of isolation.

The approach was methodical, a testament to an intelligence that understood the strategic importance of crippled infrastructure. Individual hornet squads, each comprised of dozens of colossal stinging insects, fanned out from their hidden staging grounds. Their flight paths were not random. They followed pre-determined vectors, guided by the scouts and the intricate mapping of human vulnerabilities. Their sheer bulk, easily twice the size of any native insect, made them impossible to ignore once they were in sight. Yet, their stealth in approaching these vital installations was uncanny, their massive forms blending with the deepening shadows of dawn, their wingbeats a muffled thrum against the rising cacophony of the agricultural hub's operational failures.

One such squad, led by a seasoned warrior hornet whose mandibles bore the scars of countless skirmishes, approached a key communications array. This tower, a lattice of steel reaching hundreds of feet into the sky, was a vital hub for regional data transmission. Its base was surrounded by a perimeter fence, guarded by automated sentry turrets, a testament to human paranoia. But paranoia had not accounted for an enemy that could simply fly over, or, more precisely, beneath the effective range of their terrestrial defenses.

The hornets didn't land directly on the tower. Instead, they targeted the massive, insulated cables that snaked away from its base, carrying the vital signals towards the wider network. With a precision that belied their fearsome appearance, the hornets descended. Their powerful jaws, capable of shearing through wood and bone, went to work on the thick, protective sheathing of the cables. It wasn't just a random act of destruction; it was a calculated dismantling. They severed the cables one by one, their massive bodies working in unison, a terrifying choreography of destruction. The sound of their mandibles gnawing through the synthetic material was like a metallic rasp, a sound that would soon become synonymous with despair.

The disruption was immediate. Across the region, communication lines flickered and died. The coordinated efforts of human emergency services, already hampered by the earlier sabotage, ground to a halt. Control centers were suddenly isolated, their directives unable to reach their intended destinations. The fog of war, so to speak, was descending, thick and suffocating.

Another hornet unit was dispatched to a regional power substation, a sprawling complex of transformers and pylons that supplied electricity to the agricultural hub and the surrounding communities. Their objective was not to cause a widespread blackout, that would come later, but to create a precise, localized disruption that would sow further chaos. They targeted the high-voltage transmission lines, the thick, arcing conduits that carried the lifeblood of human industry.

Here, their natural armament was employed with devastating effect. The murder hornets, renowned for their potent venom, unleashed it not in a stinging attack on a living target, but as a directed spray onto the insulators that protected the live wires. The venom, a complex cocktail of neurotoxins and corrosive agents, was highly conductive and incredibly destructive to the materials used in electrical insulation. As the venom spread, it created micro-fractures, weakening the protective layers and, more critically, increasing the conductivity of the entire system.

The results were dramatic. Sparks began to arc violently between the towers, illuminating the pre-dawn sky with a sinister, flickering light. Transformers overloaded, their hum escalating to a tortured whine before they exploded in showers of sparks and molten metal. The localized blackout that ensued plunged the immediate vicinity into darkness, amplifying the fear and confusion already gripping the inhabitants of the agricultural hub. This was not a brute-force attack; it was an intelligent, targeted strike designed to cripple the very systems that underpinned human society.

The sheer size of the hornets was a weapon in itself, a visual terror that would fuel the growing panic. Unlike the swarming masses of smaller insects, the murder hornets were individual predators, each a formidable threat. Their wingspans, stretching to several inches, made them appear like monstrous airborne machines. Their segmented bodies, encased in chitinous armor, radiated an aura of raw power. Their compound eyes, multifaceted and predatory, seemed to absorb the dim light, reflecting a chilling, alien awareness.

As the human technicians, alerted by the catastrophic failures, scrambled to assess the damage, they were met with a sight that defied all comprehension. Giant, predatory insects were actively dismantling their infrastructure. The reports that trickled in were disjointed, fragmented, filled with disbelief and raw terror. "They're huge," one technician stammered over a failing radio link. "Like... flying tanks. And they're eating the wires." Another, his voice choked with fear, described a hornet hovering directly in front of his face, its mandibles clicking, its venom dripping onto the concrete below.

The hornets, however, were not engaging in random acts of violence. Their aggression was focused, their objective clear. They were disruptors, shock troops tasked with creating an environment of overwhelming chaos and disabling human response capabilities. They were the visible, terrifying manifestation of the unseen war that was already underway.

Their ferocity was not born of mindless rage, but of a primal, directed fury, amplified by the strategic imperative laid out by Vespida.

The effectiveness of their attacks was amplified by the coordinated efforts of the other insect factions. While the hornets severed communication and power lines, the fire ants were busy contaminating food stores and disrupting ground transportation, and the solitary wasps were disabling machinery deep within the processing plants. The human response was being systematically dismantled on multiple fronts, each strike contributing to a growing sense of helplessness.

The sheer physical presence of the murder hornets served as a psychological weapon. Their ability to fly, to move with relative impunity through the airspace, offered no sanctuary. They were a constant, terrifying reminder that the human world, so carefully constructed and controlled, was now vulnerable to forces beyond their understanding and their capacity to retaliate effectively. The days of humans being the apex predators, the unquestioned rulers of the terrestrial domain, were rapidly drawing to a close.

As the sun climbed higher, casting its stark light on the scene of destruction, the murder hornets began to withdraw, their initial objectives met. They did not linger, did not engage in unnecessary confrontation. Their role was to strike hard, to disrupt, and to create the conditions for the next phase of the offensive. They left behind a landscape scarred by their passage, a testament to their destructive power and their chilling strategic acumen. The communications grid was in tatters, the power supply fractured, and the psychological impact on the human population was immense. The first strike had indeed been a success, and the murder hornets, as the vanguard of Vespida's forces, had proven themselves to be the terrifying embodiment of nature's wrath, a visceral preview of the war to come. Their sting was not just venomous; it was a declaration of war, a thunderous pronouncement that the age of insect subjugation was over, and the era of insect dominion had begun. The very air crackled with the aftermath of their assault, a silent scream from the broken technological arteries of the human world. The terror they inspired was not merely a byproduct of their ferocity; it was a carefully cultivated weapon, designed to sow seeds of doubt and fear, to paralyze the enemy before the true battle even began. Their mission was complete, but the impact of their devastating work would echo for days to come, a stark reminder of the power that lay dormant, now awakened and directed by a singular, unified will.

The rumble of the emergency generators was a hollow sound, a desperate heartbeat against the encroaching silence. While the murder hornets had delivered the decapitating blows to communication and power grids, the true insidious rot began to spread from below, a creeping paralysis driven by an enemy far smaller, yet no less deadly. The fire ants, a crimson tide of relentless purpose, had already begun their burrowing insurrection, their tiny mandibles proving more effective than any explosive charge against the intricate sinews of human infrastructure.

Their campaign was a masterclass in subterranean warfare, a symphony of unseen destruction orchestrated by an ancient, primal intelligence. It wasn't enough for them to simply swarm; they infiltrated, they insinuated, they dissolved the very foundations of the agricultural hub's operations from within. Their initial incursions were subtle, almost imperceptible. As the automated systems faltered and the human response teams grappled with the airborne assault, the ants were already deep within the bowels of the complex. They sought out the access points, the service tunnels, the forgotten conduits that laced the earth beneath the gleaming metal and concrete.

Their primary targets were the lifeblood of any complex machinery: lubrication systems, coolant conduits, and intricate hydraulic lines. Imagine a vast, complex organism; the ants were the microscopic parasites, finding their way into the arteries and veins, clogging them, corroding them, poisoning them. They didn't chew through thick metal casings directly, not at first. Their strength lay in precision and persistence. They found the minute imperfections, the hairline cracks in seals, the slightly loosened fittings, the microscopic gaps where water or oil might slowly seep. Into these, they poured.

The sheer density of their numbers was their first overwhelming weapon. A single ant might be insignificant, but a million, a billion, working in concert, became an irresistible force. They moved with a unified, instinctual drive, an unbroken stream flowing towards the critical systems. They would engulf valves, their tiny bodies creating a living seal that prevented movement, their collective weight a subtle pressure that could warp delicate mechanisms. They burrowed into the very insulation of electrical wiring, not to sever it, but to create micro-short circuits, a slow drain of power that could manifest as erratic behavior in sensitive control panels, or, worse, a spontaneous combustion in a critical junction box.

Consider the hydraulic systems that controlled the massive conveyor belts, the automated harvest machinery, the intricate climate control units essential for the seed banks. These systems relied on high-pressure fluid, a precisely balanced mix of oil and additives. The fire ants, with an almost uncanny understanding of chemistry, began to contaminate this fluid. They carried with them not just their own pheromones and waste products, but also microscopic fragments of the materials they encountered – dust, grit, and even tiny shards of corroded metal. These foreign contaminants, introduced into the pressurized lines, acted like grit in a finely tuned engine. They abraded seals, clogged filters, and introduced imbalances into the fluid dynamics. The result was a gradual, but inevitable, degradation of performance.

Conveyor belts that had once moved with smooth efficiency began to shudder, to seize, their motors straining against an unseen resistance. Automated harvesters, designed to pluck delicate fruits with surgical precision, started to crush them, their hydraulic arms responding sluggishly, erratically, to commands that were themselves being corrupted by the failing systems. The delicate dance of automated agriculture was being reduced to a series of jerky, destructive spasms.

Water purification systems, vital for the vast hydroponic farms and the sustenance of the human population within the hub, also became a primary target. The ants didn't just contaminate; they burrowed into the very membranes and filters of these systems. Their nests, often constructed with surprising speed and tenacity, were built within the filtration units themselves. The fine particles they used in nest construction, combined with their own excretions, rapidly clogged the delicate pores of the filters, rendering them useless. The clean water flowing into the hub began to carry with it a subtle, acrid taste, a hint of the subterranean invasion. Tests that were still functioning registered abnormalities, but the sheer volume of incoming data, already compromised by the communication failures, made it difficult to isolate the source of the contamination.

The electronic heart of the hub, the complex network of sensors, processors, and control modules that governed everything from crop yields to environmental stability, was particularly vulnerable to this type of infestation. The ants, in their relentless quest for nesting material and optimal living conditions, would burrow into the ventilation systems of server rooms, seeking out the warmth generated by the machinery.

Their sheer numbers would overwhelm the air filters, coating sensitive circuit boards with a fine layer of dust and chitin. Worse, they would forge new pathways, chewing through the delicate insulation of wires, creating unintended connections and short circuits that sent erratic signals through the network.

Imagine a single, crucial circuit board, its pathways like miniature highways carrying vital information. Now imagine millions of tiny ants marching across it, their antennae brushing against components, their bodies creating a conductive bridge between previously isolated points. A signal meant for one processor would be diverted, a command intended for a specific actuator would be rerouted, or, most disastrously, a critical data packet would be lost entirely, corrupted by the mere presence of the infestation.

This was not a battle that could be fought with conventional weaponry. How does one deploy a flamethrower against an enemy that operates beneath the ground, within the very walls and conduits of your own facilities? How do you target an enemy that uses the very infrastructure you rely on as its highway and its fortress? The ants were the ultimate infiltrators, the embodiment of the saying that a small leak can sink a great ship. Their invasion was a slow, insidious poison, working its way into the system, weakening it from within, and rendering the more visible, spectacular attacks of the hornets and wasps all the more devastating.

The human technicians, already stretched thin and disoriented by the larger-scale disruptions, found themselves facing a maddening array of minor, yet critical, failures. A valve here refused to close, a sensor there gave a nonsensical reading, a conveyor belt intermittently seized, causing cascading delays. Each incident, in isolation, seemed explainable by mechanical failure or simple wear and tear. But the sheer volume of these small, persistent problems, the way they seemed to multiply and spread, hinted at a deeper, more pervasive issue.

The ants were the silent majority of Vespida's invading force, their relentless, unglamorous work forming the bedrock of the enemy's strategy. They were the saboteurs, the contaminators, the unseen saboteurs who ensured that even if a system could be repaired, it would likely fail again, or that the repaired component would be immediately compromised by the pervasive infestation. Their understanding of the physical world, of the interconnectedness of systems, was profound. They intuitively grasped that true dominance wasn't about brute force, but about dismantling the enemy's support structure, about introducing a subtle, persistent decay that would eventually lead to collapse.

The ground beneath the agricultural hub was no longer just soil and rock; it was a vast, interconnected ant colony, a hidden network of tunnels and chambers that pulsed with a unified, destructive intent. Every service tunnel was a potential highway, every ventilation shaft a route to a vital system. They were the "ants in the machine," the unseen workers whose diligence and sheer numbers were systematically dismantling the intricate clockwork of human control. The terror they inspired was not the immediate shock of a hornet's sting, but the gnawing dread of an inevitable, unseen decay, a realization that the enemy was not just outside, but already inside, working from the very heart of their world. The infrastructure, so meticulously designed and maintained, was proving to be more of a vulnerability than a strength, a complex labyrinth easily exploited by an enemy that understood the power of the small, the persistent, and the deeply embedded. The dawn had broken not just on a ruined sky, but on a world where the ground itself had become an enemy, teeming with life that was systematically unmaking civilization, one tiny, determined burrow at a time.

The initial shockwave of the fire ant insurrection had barely subsided, the creeping dread of subterranean sabotage solidifying into a grim reality, when the skies unleashed their own special brand of hell. The murder hornets, a terror that had already proven capable of shredding communication lines and sowing widespread panic, were not the only aerial threat. A different, more ubiquitous, yet equally lethal force was preparing to descend, a buzzing, chitinous storm that would seal the agricultural hub's fate not with surgical precision, but with sheer, overwhelming force of numbers. The killer bees, a breed mutated by the very environmental collapse they now amplified, were the next phase of Vespida's multi-pronged assault.

Their arrival wasn't heralded by the deep, guttural hum of the hornets, but by a rising crescendo of high-pitched whines, a sound that began as a distant thrum and rapidly escalated into an unbearable, omnipresent shriek. It was the sound of millions upon millions of tiny wings, beating in unison, a living, breathing entity that blotted out the sun. The air itself seemed to thicken, saturated with their frantic energy. For the beleaguered humans caught in the open, it was an immediate and terrifying immersion into a nightmare of buzzing death.

The killer bees were not subtle. Unlike the ants that worked in the shadows, dismantling the infrastructure from beneath, the bees operated in plain sight, their strategy a brutal, overwhelming application of swarm tactics. Their objective was not to disable machines, but to disable the operators, to turn the very act of survival into a desperate, losing battle against an enemy that permeated every inch of the environment. They were the ultimate living blockade, a biological wall designed to prevent any coherent human response, any organized counter-attack.

The first wave descended upon the perimeter patrols, the brave but ultimately futile attempts to re-establish a cordon around the embattled hub. These were the soldiers, the engineers, the first responders who had ventured out, their faces grim, their equipment tested but not yet truly broken. For them, the sky turned into a kaleidoscope of darting, venomous projectiles. The bees moved with an unnerving coordination, a terrifying display of unified purpose that belied their individual insignificance. They didn't just fly randomly; they dove.

It began with a few scattered attacks, a probing action to gauge the enemy's defenses. A lone engineer, checking a damaged sensor array outside the main perimeter, found himself suddenly engulfed. It wasn't a single sting, but a hundred, a thousand, all at once. The bees, drawn by the heat, the movement, the very scent of human life, converged on him with astonishing speed. His protective gear, designed to withstand the occasional hornet sting, offered little resistance to the sheer volume of attackers. The bees found the microscopic gaps, the seams where fabric met visor, the minuscule openings at the gloves. They poured in, their stingers injecting potent neurotoxins and cytotoxins into his exposed skin, into his lungs, into his very being. His screams were quickly muffled by the deafening drone, his struggles becoming increasingly frantic and ineffective against the ceaseless onslaught.

Then, the barrage intensified. The coordinated dives began. Entire squadrons of bees, thousands strong, would peel away from the main swarm, a dark, undulating wave that plummeted towards the ground. They targeted anything that moved, anything that represented a threat or a potential food source. The armored vehicles, designed to withstand kinetic impacts, suddenly found themselves under a different kind of siege. The bees would swarm over the chassis, their bodies obscuring vision, their stingers finding the tiny cracks in the armor, the seals around windows, the vents. While the thick plating might offer some protection against individual stings, the sheer density of the attack was overwhelming.

Imagine a soldier inside one of these vehicles. The interior, already tense and claustrophobic, would become a suffocating inferno of buzzing. The bees, attracted by the warmth and the carbon dioxide exhaled by the occupants, would find their way through any available aperture. They would flood the cabin, their stings finding the unprotected flesh of faces, hands, and necks. The driver, struggling to maintain control, would be incapacitated by a hail of venom, his vision blurred, his motor functions failing. The vehicle itself would become a death trap, the enclosed space amplifying the terror and the lethality of the infestation.

One particular incident highlighted the terrifying effectiveness of their numbers. A small reconnaissance team, attempting to assess the damage to a vital water pipeline several kilometers from the hub, found themselves cut off. Their all-terrain vehicles, robust and well-equipped, were their only hope of escape. As they tried to navigate the debris-strewn landscape, the killer bees descended. The sky, already a murky gray from the ongoing environmental degradation, turned a living black as the swarm enveloped them.

The vehicles' thermal imaging systems, designed to detect enemy combatants, were now overwhelmed by the heat signatures of the bees, painting the screens with a uniform, terrifying orange glow. The lead vehicle, attempting to accelerate away, was immediately targeted. The bees, like a viscous liquid, coated its windscreen, rendering it completely blind. They massed on the engine vents, their bodies creating a biological heat sink, suffocating the machinery. Within moments, the engine sputtered and died, leaving the vehicle stranded.

The second vehicle, seeing the fate of the first, attempted a flanking maneuver. This was precisely what the bees were anticipating. They shifted their focus, a vast, undulating mass that flowed with terrifying speed. The flanking vehicle, caught in the open, became the epicenter of the swarm. The driver, trying to swerve, lost control as a concentrated wave of bees hit the windshield, shattering the reinforced glass and entering the cabin in a blinding fury. The screams from within were cut short by the relentless, high-pitched drone.

The third vehicle, the only one remaining, was a transport carrying vital medical supplies. Its occupants, desperate to escape, tried to use their limited defensive countermeasures. They deployed a sonic deterrent, a device designed to emit frequencies that would repel insects. For a fleeting moment, it seemed to work, creating a small pocket of relative calm around the vehicle. But the bees, far from being deterred, seemed to be agitated by the sound. The swarm fractured, then reformed, converging with an even greater ferocity. The sonic device, likely damaged by the vibrations or simply overwhelmed by the sheer density of the attackers, began to malfunction, emitting a distorted, screeching noise that only seemed to draw more of the deadly insects.

The scenario repeated itself across the entire perimeter. Any attempt to move, any sign of organized human activity, was met with an immediate, overwhelming response from the killer bee swarms. They acted as a living, buzzing blockade, their relentless swarming tactics designed not just to kill, but to incapacitate, to disorient, and to demoralize. The chaos they generated was immense. Personnel trying to repair damaged infrastructure found themselves forced to abandon their tasks, their protective suits a flimsy barrier against the venomous rain. Communication attempts were hampered by the sheer noise and the constant threat of attack, turning any open-air conversation into a death sentence.

The bees' coordinated dives weren't just random acts of aggression; they were calculated strikes. They targeted exposed limbs, faces, and any areas where their stingers could penetrate with maximum effect. The venom itself was a potent cocktail, a paralytic agent that could quickly overwhelm the nervous system. But it was the sheer volume that truly broke the human spirit. Imagine being pummeled by thousands of tiny, venomous projectiles, each one injecting a burning dose of toxin. The pain was excruciating, but the psychological toll was even greater. The constant, inescapable buzz was a maddening symphony of impending doom.

The impact on the agricultural hub's operations was catastrophic. The planned evacuation routes were instantly rendered impassable. The repair crews, already struggling with the ant infestations and the damage from the initial hornet attacks, were now facing a completely new and devastating threat. The automated systems, some of which had managed to remain partially operational despite the ant infiltration, were also vulnerable. Drones, attempting reconnaissance or delivery missions, were swarmed and brought crashing down, their delicate components a playground for the marauding insects.

The killer bees were the perfect complement to the fire ants. While the ants worked insidiously to dismantle the hub from within, the bees ensured that no organized human intervention could effectively counter their subterranean allies. They created a battlefield of pure sensory overload, a terrifying testament to the power of unbridled numbers and instinctual, terrifying coordination. The sheer visual spectacle of the swarms, the deafening drone, the pervasive scent of venom in the air – it all conspired to break the will of the defenders.

In the face of such overwhelming force, such absolute dominion of the air, any organized resistance crumbled. The human defenders, reduced to a state of desperate survival, were forced to retreat into the most heavily fortified sections of the hub, abandoning the outer defenses and leaving large swathes of the complex vulnerable to further infestation and destruction. The killer bee barrage had effectively sealed their fate, transforming the agricultural hub from a beacon of human resilience into a besieged fortress, its occupants trapped within walls that were rapidly becoming their tomb, under skies that belonged to the swarm. The message was clear: Vespida's conquest was not a matter of if, but when, and the buzzing legions of the killer bees were the harbingers of its inevitable, terrifying conclusion.

The skies had become a canvas of terror, painted with the relentless, high-pitched whine of countless wings. While the overwhelming mass of killer bees had already achieved a devastating paralysis of human defenses, a subtler, yet equally insidious, component of Vespida's assault was now being deployed: the wasps. Not the colossal, brute-force hornets that had previously demonstrated their capacity for destruction, nor the sheer overwhelming numbers of the killer bee swarms, but a different breed, smaller, faster, and far more cunning. These were the reconnaissance units, the psychological shock troops, tasked with a mission of observation and terror.

Their arrival was not marked by the deafening crescendo that had accompanied the bees, but by a series of sharp, piercing shrieks that sliced through the existing cacophony. These were the specialized scout wasps, their movements impossibly quick, their flight patterns erratic and unpredictable. They darted and weaved through the air, appearing and disappearing with unnerving alacrity, like living, venomous specters. Their primary objective was not to engage in prolonged, direct combat, but to gather vital intelligence, to catalog human reactions, to map troop movements, and to identify vulnerabilities with a precision that belied their insectile nature.

One could observe them hovering near the edges of the besieged agricultural hub, their multifaceted eyes scanning the terrain, their antennae twitching, absorbing every nuance of the unfolding chaos. They would approach the periphery of fortified positions, their flight paths deliberately erratic, designed to draw attention, to provoke a response. A sudden burst of defensive fire from a human position would elicit a flurry of activity from these scouts. They would peel away, not in retreat, but to relay the information, to observe the trajectory of projectiles, the speed of vehicle deployments, the effectiveness of countermeasures. It was a silent, deadly game of cat and mouse, played out against a backdrop of unimaginable carnage.

Their venom was not solely designed for immediate lethality, though it certainly possessed that capability. Instead, it was a potent neurotoxin, capable of inducing intense pain, disorientation, and debilitating fear. A single sting, even through rudimentary protective gear, could send a shockwave of agony through a victim, clouding judgment and sowing seeds of panic. This was their secondary, and arguably more devastating, objective: psychological warfare. They were the architects of fear, the instruments of despair.

Witness the scenario of a small contingent of human defenders attempting to consolidate their positions within a partially collapsed building. As they worked to barricade a shattered entrance, a few of these scout wasps would appear, their approach swift and silent, until the last moment. They would dive, not at the group, but at individuals, targeting exposed skin or any infinitesimal gap in their armor. A technician, his hands busy with reinforcing a metal plate, might feel a searing lance of pain in his forearm. The initial shock would be visceral, followed by a rapid onset of muscle spasms and a disorienting dizziness. The venom, designed for psychological impact, would begin its insidious work.

The victim, writhing in agony, would cry out, attracting the attention of his comrades. This was precisely the desired effect. The other defenders, already on edge, their nerves frayed by the incessant drone of the killer bees and the memory of the hornet attacks, would be instantly on high alert. Their focus would shift from the immediate task of defense to the immediate threat of further wasp attacks. They would scan the skies, their movements becoming more hesitant, their coordination faltering. The scout wasps, having achieved their initial objective, would dart away, leaving behind a trail of fear and confusion, their mission of destabilization already in motion.

These wasps were not indiscriminate in their attacks. They displayed an uncanny ability to identify targets that would have the greatest psychological impact. A lone sentinel on watch, his face etched with exhaustion, might be the target of a swift, venomous strike. The resulting scream, amplified by the confined space, would shatter the fragile composure of those around him. The venom's paralytic properties would begin to set in, making escape or effective self-defense nearly impossible. The remaining defenders would be forced to choose between aiding their fallen comrade, a perilous undertaking given the wasps' continued aerial presence, or abandoning him to his fate to preserve their own lives. This forced dichotomy of loyalty versus survival was a potent tool in Vespida's arsenal, designed to erode trust and foster a sense of helplessness.

Their movements were a masterful display of aerial reconnaissance. They would patrol the perimeter of the surviving human strongholds, their routes meticulously mapped and constantly updated. They observed the flow of personnel, the deployment of resources, the attempts to repair damaged infrastructure. They noted the patterns of defensive fire, the blind spots in surveillance, the moments of vulnerability. This intelligence, relayed through an unseen network – perhaps pheromonal signals or sonic frequencies imperceptible to human ears – would be fed back to the larger Vespida command, guiding the actions of the more destructive forces.

Imagine a team of engineers, attempting to restore power

to a critical section of the hub. They would work under the oppressive shadow of the bee swarms, their movements slow and deliberate, their protective suits bulky and cumbersome. As they neared the damaged generator, a pair of scout wasps would materialize from the hazy sky. They wouldn't attack directly, not initially. Instead, they would hover, their bodies impossibly still against the swirling air, their predatory gaze fixed on the humans. The engineers, acutely aware of the constant threat, would feel their anxiety amplify. Their movements would become more hurried, more prone to error. The wasps would then execute a series of rapid, feinting maneuvers, circling the engineers, their venomous stingers glinting.

One engineer, perhaps distracted by a sudden, unnerving buzz close to his ear, might flinch. This micro-movement, this subtle shift in his posture, would be all the scout wasps needed. In a blur of motion, they would descend. One would sting his exposed hand, the venom instantly coursing through his veins, causing a blinding pain and involuntary tremors. The other wasp might focus its attack on his head, aiming for the vulnerable gap between his helmet and his respirator. The immediate consequence would be a piercing scream, a cascade of dropped tools, and the immediate cessation of all work. The other engineers, witnessing this swift, brutal incapacitation, would likely freeze, their morale shattered, their resolve crumbling. The scout wasps, having successfully disrupted the operation and inflicted casualties, would then retreat, leaving the scene a tableau of broken efforts and heightened terror.

The psychological toll of these wasp patrols was immense. The constant, unpredictable threat of their attacks meant that no moment of relative calm could ever be truly trusted. Every shadow could conceal a hunter, every sudden movement in the periphery could signal an impending strike. This pervasive sense of unease, of being perpetually under surveillance and vulnerable to swift, agonizing attack, wore down the human defenders. Sleep became a luxury, rest a dangerous indulgence. The human psyche, already strained by the overwhelming scale of the disaster, began to fracture under the relentless pressure.

Furthermore, the scout wasps played a crucial role in amplifying the terror of the other Vespida forces. Their darting, aggressive movements, often preceding a larger swarm or a coordinated hornet strike, served as an early warning system, but one laced with dread. The sight of these agile predators would trigger a primal fear, a visceral understanding that something worse was about to follow. They were the advance agents of chaos, heralding the arrival of Vespida's more overt instruments of destruction.

The human command structure, already struggling to coordinate a defense against multiple simultaneous threats, found itself increasingly crippled by the reconnaissance activities of these wasps. Attempts to redeploy forces were often met with unexpected resistance, as the scout wasps, having observed the movement patterns, would guide other Vespida units to intercept. Communication lines, already tenuous, were further strained as personnel became hesitant to venture into open areas for fear of wasp ambushes, vital information thus failing to reach its intended destinations.

The strategic implication of the wasp reconnaissance was profound. It allowed Vespida to adapt its tactics in real-time, to exploit weaknesses as they appeared, and to maintain a constant pressure on the beleaguered human forces. They were not simply insects; they were intelligent, adaptive scouts, operating with a chilling efficiency that underscored the sophisticated nature of Vespida's assault. The buzzing drone of the killer bees had already instilled a sense of overwhelming dread, but the sharp, piercing shrieks and the lightning-fast strikes of the scout wasps added a layer of deeply personal terror, a constant reminder of the pervasive and inescapable nature of their enemy. The environment itself had become a weapon, and these wasps were its most precise and venomous instruments.

Humanity's Stand

HUMANITY'S RECKONING

The initial days after the first, localized incidents were characterized by a profound, almost willful, disbelief. From the comfort of their climate-controlled environments, news anchors, their faces meticulously made up to project an aura of calm authority, reported on bizarre, isolated events. Tales of inexplicable swarms descending upon remote farms, of highways grinding to a halt under impossible densities of winged creatures, of inexplicable livestock deaths attributed to everything from new strains of avian flu to mass hysteria. The language used was deliberately downplayed: "unusual insect activity," "localized environmental anomalies," "unconfirmed reports."

Governments, caught flat-footed and utterly unprepared for anything remotely resembling the reality, issued statements that were a masterclass in evasion. Official communiqués spoke of coordinated efforts to understand and contain these "phenomena," employing jargon designed to reassure without actually conveying any concrete information. The underlying sentiment, broadcast through carefully worded press conferences and leaked "expert opinions," was that these were merely isolated outbreaks, perhaps triggered by unusual weather patterns or human industrial negligence. The idea that these were organized, directed attacks by sentient, or at least intelligently coordinated, insectoid entities was simply too outlandish to be entertained, even by those directly witnessing the unfolding horror.

In the burgeoning internet forums and shadowy corners of the digital world, however, a different narrative was beginning to coalesce. Whispers of "Vespida," a term coined by anonymous users piecing together fragments of scientific research suppressed for decades, began to circulate. These were dismissed by the mainstream as conspiracy theories, the ramblings of the paranoid and the delusional. Yet, for those who had seen the impossible – the precision of the hornet formations, the unnerving intelligence in the eyes of a queen wasp observing a battlefield, the sheer, suffocating dread of a killer bee swarm that seemed to possess a singular, malevolent purpose – these whispers held a terrifying resonance.

Sarah Jenkins, a renowned entomologist whose work on insect communication had been largely ignored by the scientific establishment, found herself at the epicenter of this dawning realization. For years, she had been a Cassandra, her warnings about the potential for Vespida's manipulation of insect behavior dismissed as alarmist fantasy. Now, her fragmented research papers, previously relegated to obscure academic journals, were being unearthed and disseminated with a desperate urgency. She recalled a specific instance, early in her career, when she had presented findings on the complex chemical signaling pathways that could, hypothetically, be hijacked to control vast insect populations. Her colleagues had politely, but firmly, suggested she focus on more "practical" applications. The sheer audacity of the idea – that the intricate dance of pheromones and environmental cues could be weaponized on a global scale – had been beyond their comprehension.

The initial news coverage was a surreal mosaic of denial and confusion. A report from a rural farming community in Kansas described an entire harvest being obliterated overnight by what appeared to be a hyper-aggressive strain of locusts, yet the accompanying visuals showed winged creatures far too large and uniformly aggressive to be any known species. Another broadcast from a coastal city detailed a sudden and inexplicable infestation of massive, iridescent beetles that swarmed over a naval base, disabling critical electronic systems with an unnerving precision. The military's response was equally muddled. Initial attempts to deploy conventional pest control measures proved laughably ineffective, if not disastrously counterproductive. Ground troops, accustomed to facing human adversaries with predictable tactics, were utterly disoriented by an enemy that could literally blot out the sun, an enemy that moved with a terrifying, alien logic.

The disconnect between the reality on the ground and the official narrative was stark. While families huddled in their homes, listening to the ominous hum of unseen swarms and the chilling shriek of scouts, the government insisted that the situation was under control. This public reassessment of reality, this forced confrontation with the inadequacy of human understanding, was as devastating as the physical attacks themselves. Centuries of human dominance, of seeing nature as something to be cataloged, controlled, and exploited, had bred a deep-seated arrogance. The notion that the planet's most numerous inhabitants, creatures long relegated to the realm of pests and nuisctions, could orchestrate an existential threat was an affront to the very core of human self-perception.

Consider the plight of the emergency services in the early days. Paramedics, responding to reports of mass panic attacks or unexplained allergic reactions, found themselves confronting victims not just in shock, but in physical agony from venom they couldn't identify. Their hazmat suits, designed for chemical spills, offered little protection against the microscopic barbs and potent neurotoxins being deployed with such terrifying efficacy. The sheer volume of calls quickly overwhelmed their capacity, leaving entire communities isolated and vulnerable. The dispatchers, bombarded with increasingly frantic and often nonsensical reports, struggled to prioritize, their understanding of the threat evolving from mundane emergencies to something far more terrifying with each passing minute.

One dispatch recording, later leaked and disseminated across the nascent underground information networks, captured this agonizing transition. The voice of a young dispatcher, initially calm and professional, began to crack as the calls grew more desperate. "...and they're saying the whole sky is black, ma'am, with...

insects? Are you sure about that? Could you describe them?" A pause, then a stifled gasp. "Oh my god... my God, they're inside the building... No! Get away from the window! What do you mean, 'the windows are melting'?" The recording cut off abruptly, leaving only the crackle of static and the chilling implication of what had transpired.

The media, caught between a desire to report the truth and immense pressure from authorities to maintain a semblance of order, struggled to reconcile the fragmented accounts. Editorials debated the psychological impact of widespread fear, suggesting mass delusion. Experts, often chosen for their adherence to conventional entomological doctrine rather than their willingness to consider the unbelievable, appeared on television to offer rational explanations, theories that crumbled like sandcastles against the rising tide of empirical evidence. This internal conflict within the human information apparatus was a critical vulnerability. It fostered doubt, eroded trust, and ultimately, delayed the unified response that was so desperately needed.

The initial government response was characterized by a profound miscalculation of the enemy's capabilities. When reports of coordinated hornet attacks began to surface, the immediate reaction was to deploy conventional anti-air measures. Fighter jets scrambled, missile systems were activated, and troops were mobilized to establish perimeters. However, the sheer scale and adaptability of Vespida's forces rendered these efforts futile. The hornets, with their astonishing agility and their ability to break into smaller, unpredictable formations, proved incredibly difficult targets for conventional weaponry. Missiles often detonated in empty air, while the rapid-fire cannon of jets could only thin the edges of a swarm that seemed to regenerate itself from the sky. The frustration of the military was palpable, a growing realization that their advanced technology was being rendered obsolete by an enemy that possessed neither sophisticated hardware nor complex logistical chains, at least not in any way humans understood.

Even more baffling was the initial reaction to the killer bees. Their sheer numbers were so overwhelming, so fundamentally beyond any previously conceived biological threat, that many simply refused to believe it. The concept of trillions of individual organisms acting in perfect unison, capable of sophisticated coordinated attacks, was a bridge too far for most rational minds. Initial analyses focused on environmental factors, on unusual migration patterns, on the possibility of a viral mutation affecting bee behavior on an unprecedented scale. The notion that these were not merely bees, but meticulously controlled biological weapons, remained largely outside the realm of serious consideration for weeks, even months, after the first catastrophic impacts.

The economic ramifications were equally ignored in the early stages. As transportation networks began to falter under the sheer density of insect life, and agricultural output plummeted due to targeted destruction of crops and pollinators, the global markets remained stubbornly resistant to acknowledging the true nature of the crisis. Analysts spoke of temporary disruptions, of supply chain issues, of a "global agricultural slowdown." The idea that the very foundations of the global economy were being systematically dismantled by an enemy that cared nothing for market values or currency was simply not factored into their models. This economic denial, this adherence to old paradigms, only deepened the eventual collapse.

Within the scientific community, a silent schism began to form. The vast majority, bound by decades of established research and professional inertia, continued to dismiss the increasingly alarming reports. They clung to familiar classifications and evolutionary pathways, unable to accommodate the radical departure that Vespida represented. A smaller, more intrepid group, however, began to cautiously entertain the unthinkable. These were the researchers who had, in their own quiet ways, already been pushing the boundaries of understanding insect intelligence and behavior. They recognized in the early reports echoes of their own radical hypotheses, the unsettling confirmations of their deepest fears.

Dr. Aris Thorne, a leading theoretical biologist who had spent his career studying emergent intelligence in complex systems, found himself ostracized for daring to suggest a unifying, non-natural cause. He published a paper, initially intended for a specialized symposium, outlining a framework for understanding Vespida as a networked, self-organizing intelligence that leveraged biological organisms as its agents. The paper was met with derision, accusations of sensationalism, and in some cases, outright professional condemnation. The prevailing sentiment was that Thorne was allowing his imagination to run away with him, that he was conflating complex biological phenomena with sentient intent. He was accused of anthropomorphizing the insect world, of projecting human concepts of warfare onto a natural system.

The authorities, meanwhile, remained locked in a cycle of reactive measure and public reassurance. When a major city's power grid was crippled by a massive influx of iridescent beetles that consumed vital electrical components, the official explanation was a freak electrical storm combined with an unprecedented insect migration. When a coastal defense system was neutralized by a swarm of wasps that seemed to possess an uncanny ability to bypass electronic countermeasures, the military attributed it to a sophisticated EMP attack, not a biological one. This deliberate misdirection, this refusal to acknowledge the true enemy, was born partly of panic and partly of a desperate desire to maintain control, to prevent mass societal collapse by withholding what they deemed too terrible to be known.

The public, bombarded with contradictory information, was left adrift in a sea of uncertainty. One day, they were told the insect problem was localized; the next, they were assured that advanced containment protocols were in place. This constant flux of information, this lack of a clear, consistent narrative, bred a pervasive sense of unease, a gnawing suspicion that something vital was being withheld. It was easier, for many, to believe the comforting lies of normalcy than to confront the terrifying reality of an enemy that defied all known laws of nature and warfare. This denial was, in itself, a powerful weapon in Vespida's arsenal, allowing the initial stages of their assault to proceed with a minimum of effective resistance. The greatest threat, it turned out, was not the venom in their stingers, but the blindness in human eyes, the unwillingness to see what was undeniably, terrifyingly, there.

The sheer psychological impact of this denial cannot be overstated. For generations, humanity had viewed itself as the apex predator, the undisputed master of the natural world. The intricate, often brutal, cycles of nature were something to be observed from a distance, cataloged, and, where possible, controlled for human benefit. The idea that the planet's most ubiquitous and seemingly insignificant life forms could unite, could coordinate, could develop strategies that outmaneuvered human military might, was an existential shockwave. It shattered the very foundation of human identity.

This initial phase of disbelief and underestimation was a critical window, a period during which a unified and decisive response might have made a difference. Instead, humanity remained largely paralyzed, caught between the comforting illusions of the past and the horrifying realities of the present. The whispers of Vespida grew louder, transforming from fringe conspiracy theories into desperate pronouncements of truth, but they were still largely unheard by those in power, or worse, deliberately ignored. The stage was set for a reckoning, and humanity, blinded by its own hubris, was utterly unprepared for the curtain to rise. The enemy, it seemed, had already won the first battle, not through superior firepower, but through the sheer, overwhelming force of human denial.

The veneer of normalcy, so painstakingly maintained by media outlets and official pronouncements, began to crack with terrifying speed. What had been dismissed as isolated incidents, bizarre anomalies confined to distant news reports, rapidly bled into the fabric of everyday life. The hum, once a subtle undercurrent of distant dread, now throbbed with an amplified malevolence, a palpable presence that filled the air. The initial disbelief, a collective defense mechanism against the incomprehensible, dissolved into raw, visceral panic as the true nature of the threat became undeniable, and far more insidious than anyone could have imagined.

In the bustling heart of metropolitan centers, the morning commute, usually a predictable ballet of hurried footsteps and frustrated honking, devolved into a scene ripped from a nightmare. A sudden, localized darkening of the sky, not from clouds but from an impossibly dense mass of chitinous wings, descended upon a major transportation hub. It wasn't a gentle rain of insects; it was an invasion. The air filled with a deafening buzz, a sound that vibrated in the very bones, accompanied by the sharp, metallic clicks of countless mandibles.

Witnesses described the terror not just as a visual or auditory assault, but as a physical, suffocating weight. The sheer biomass of the swarm obscured the sun, plunging the usually bright urban landscape into an eerie twilight. People, caught in the open, were not merely inconvenienced; they were targeted. Swarms of aggressive wasps, their bodies larger than any previously documented species, descended with chilling precision, their stings delivering a potent, fast-acting neurotoxin that induced immediate paralysis and agonizing seizures. Panic erupted. Commuters, abandoning their vehicles, trampled each other in a desperate, unthinking stampede for any semblance of shelter. The orderly flow of traffic ceased, replaced by a chaotic melee of screams, the shattering of glass, and the sickening crunch of impact as fleeing crowds collided with immobile vehicles and each other.

Emergency services, already stretched thin by the initial, seemingly isolated incidents, were utterly overwhelmed. Dispatch centers became cacophonies of despair. The familiar litany of car accidents and medical emergencies was drowned out by reports of mass anaphylactic shock, inexplicable paralysis, and outright disappearances. Paramedics, struggling to navigate streets choked with abandoned vehicles and panicked throngs, found their efforts futile. Their hazmat suits, designed for chemical containment, offered scant protection against the sheer volume and insidious nature of the attack. The air itself seemed weaponized, thick with microscopic irritants and airborne toxins that bypassed even filtered breathing apparatus.

One harrowing account emerged from a children's hospital in a major city. As the first widespread swarms began to materialize, a squadron of massive, iridescent beetles, unlike any cataloged by entomologists, descended upon the building. They bypassed traditional entry points, their hard exoskeletons surprisingly adept at finding weaknesses in ventilation shafts and window seals. The children, many already weakened by illness, were plunged into unimaginable terror. Nurses and doctors, attempting to evacuate the most vulnerable, found themselves battling not only the insects but the sheer terror of the patients, a terror amplified by the sounds of the building being systematically dismantled from the outside. Reports spoke of the beetles' unsettlingly methodical approach, their focus on vital systems, on electrical conduits and structural supports, as if guided by an alien, destructive logic. The scene, as relayed in fragmented, terrified calls from hospital staff before communications went dark, painted a stark picture of civilization's fragility.

Public spaces, once symbols of human congregation and order, transformed into zones of unspeakable terror. Parks, usually vibrant with life, became death traps. A family picnic was violently interrupted by a sudden, ground-level surge of hyper-aggressive ants, their exoskeletons thick and armored, their mandibles capable of tearing through fabric and flesh with alarming ease. The ground itself seemed to writhe as the swarm, numbering in the millions, enveloped everything in its path. The screams of the victims were choked off by the sheer speed and ferocity of the attack, the onlookers frozen in a tableau of horror, too stunned and terrified to intervene.

The breakdown of civil order was not a gradual decay but an abrupt, violent rupture. As the scale of the attacks became undeniable, and official reassurances proved hollow, a primal fear took root. Looting, initially sporadic and opportunistic, became widespread. Stores were ransacked not just for supplies, but out of sheer desperation to escape the relentless onslaught. The streets, no longer patrolled by overwhelmed law enforcement, became hunting grounds. Those who had access to private vehicles attempted to flee cities, only to find escape routes choked by traffic jams and further insectoid ambushes. The psychological toll was immense; the constant awareness of being under siege, of being vulnerable to an enemy that could materialize from anywhere, at any time, pushed many to the brink of sanity.

Sarah Jenkins, watching the unfolding chaos from the relative safety of her fortified research facility, felt a chilling validation of her worst fears. The fragmented reports pouring in, the panicked broadcasts, the chilling silence from once-thriving communities – it was all precisely as she had warned. She saw footage of a national guard unit, deployed to secure a vital bridge, being overwhelmed by a relentless aerial assault of massive, venomous moths. Their advanced weaponry, their armored vehicles, were of little use against an enemy that could cloak the sky, that attacked with a disorienting swarm and potent, debilitating toxins delivered through the very air they breathed. The soldiers, trained for conventional warfare, were ill-equipped to face an enemy that operated on principles of biological warfare on a scale that defied human comprehension.

The sheer diversity of the attack was also a factor in the widespread panic. It wasn't a single type of insectoid threat, but a coordinated, multi-faceted assault. While one city might be bombarded by colossal dragonflies capable of delivering electric shocks, another would be overrun by subterranean colonies of burrowing beetles that undermined building foundations and crippled infrastructure from below. The lack of a singular, easily definable enemy only added to the confusion and terror. It was an enemy that adapted, that diversified, that seemed to learn and evolve its tactics in real-time.

The economic impact, once dismissed as temporary disruptions, now became catastrophic. Factories ground to a halt as swarms of industrial-strength parasitic mites rendered machinery inoperable or unsafe. Food processing plants were rendered useless by locusts that devoured entire stockpiles in mere hours. The global supply chain, already strained by initial disruptions, simply imploded. This economic collapse was not a consequence of war, but of nature itself seemingly rebelling, orchestrated by an unseen hand. The fragility of a civilization built on complex, interconnected systems was laid bare, revealing how quickly the pillars of modern life could crumble when faced with a sufficiently determined and overwhelming biological force.

The psychological impact was perhaps the most profound. The ingrained human belief in their dominion over nature was shattered. The smallest, most overlooked creatures had proven to be humanity's undoing. This existential crisis led to widespread existential dread. Religious institutions found themselves grappling with questions of divine wrath and the end times. Philosophers debated the very definition of sentience and intelligence, as the coordinated attacks seemed to suggest a level of collective consciousness that surpassed human understanding. The world had irrevocably changed, and the transition from disbelief to widespread terror was a brutal, rapid descent into a new, terrifying reality. The panic in the streets was merely the outward manifestation of a deeper, more insidious fear – the fear that humanity was no longer at the top of the food chain, but merely another species facing extinction.

The sterile hum of laboratory equipment, usually a comforting constant for Dr. Aris Thorne, now felt like a frantic heartbeat, mirroring the chaos unfolding outside. His sanctuary, a meticulously organized haven of petri dishes, gene sequencers, and electron microscopes, had transformed into a war room. The air was thick with the scent of ozone from overloaded equipment and the metallic tang of adrenaline. Aris, a leading entomologist whose career had been dedicated to the intricate, often overlooked world of insects, found himself at the epicenter of a biological Armageddon. His usual composure, honed by years of patient observation and meticulous data collection, was stretched thin, frayed by the sheer impossibility of it all. The data flooding in defied every established principle of entomology, every evolutionary model he had ever studied.

Across the globe, similar scenes played out. In subterranean biolabs, deep beneath the scarred surface of what was once the Amazon rainforest, xenobiologists scrambled to analyze tissue samples from colossal, bioluminescent arachnids that had emerged from the earth. Their exoskeletons pulsed with an eerie, internal light, and their venom, initially believed to be a potent neurotoxin, was now showing evidence of complex protein structures capable of cellular regeneration – for the arachnids themselves. In the frozen wastes of Siberia, cryo-entomologists worked against the clock, attempting to understand the adaptation of arctic invertebrates that had suddenly developed a resistance to sub-zero temperatures, and worse, an aggressive territoriality towards any mammalian life.

Aris's own lab was a microcosm of this global scientific panic. His team, comprised of brilliant minds from diverse fields – genetics, biochemistry, even theoretical physics – were locked in a desperate race against time. Dr. Lena Petrova, a geneticist whose groundbreaking work on insect pheromone communication had once earned her prestigious awards, was now staring at DNA sequences that made no sense. "It's… it's like a glitch in the code, Aris," she'd exclaimed earlier, her voice hoarse with exhaustion and disbelief. "The gene expression patterns are entirely novel. It's not just adaptation; it's an active, directed rewrite. As if they're consciously editing their own biological blueprints."

The initial assumption had been environmental catastrophe – a runaway mutation caused by pollutants, radiation, or some unknown atmospheric change. But the sheer coordination, the apparent sentience, argued against random chance. The way the swarms moved with unified intent, the uncanny intelligence displayed in their attacks, pointed towards something far more profound, and terrifying. It was as if the very ecosystems, driven to the brink by humanity's relentless exploitation, had finally spawned a collective consciousness, a planet-wide immune response orchestrated by its smallest inhabitants.

"We're still trying to isolate the primary trigger," reported Ben Carter, a young but exceptionally gifted biochemist, his face illuminated by the flickering glow of a mass spectrometer. "We've identified complex signaling molecules, unlike any known neurotransmitters or hormones. They're transmitting information at a speed that bypasses conventional biological pathways. It's almost... digital."

Aris stared at the holographic projection of a honeybee's brain, its intricate neural network rendered in shimmering blue light. Their most recent data suggested that the insects weren't just acting on instinct; they were communicating, strategizing, learning. The 'hive mind' theory, once relegated to science fiction, was becoming a chillingly plausible reality. He remembered a lecture he'd given years ago, a passionate defense of the ecological importance of pollinators. He'd spoken of their intricate social structures, their efficient communication methods. He'd never imagined that their collective intelligence could evolve to this terrifying degree.

Their reliance on established scientific dogma was proving to be their greatest handicap. They were trying to understand this new paradigm using the old rules, and the rules had been rewritten by the insects themselves. The sheer diversity of the insectoid onslaught further complicated matters. Every species, from the colossal scarab beetles that burrowed through concrete to the microscopic gnats that could disable advanced electronics with their electromagnetic frequencies, seemed to operate with a shared, overarching objective.

"We're missing something fundamental," Aris mused aloud, tracing the intricate patterns on the bee's brain with a gloved finger. "We're looking for a single cause, a single mechanism. But what if it's not one thing? What if it's... everything? What if the planet itself, in its desperation, has found a way to unify its most prolific inhabitants into a single, unified defense system?"

Lena looked up from her genetic sequencer, her eyes wide with a dawning, horrifying realization. "You mean... the environmental degradation... the pollution... it didn't just

cause them to mutate. It *taught* them. It forced them to evolve this interconnectedness, this shared awareness, as a survival imperative." The implications were staggering. Humanity, in its relentless pursuit of progress, had inadvertently engineered its own extinction, not through nuclear war or asteroid impact, but by pushing the very foundations of life on Earth to their breaking point. The insects, always present, always adapting, had simply found a more effective way to survive.

Aris continued, the weight of his words settling heavily in the sterile room. "We've always viewed evolution as a slow, incremental process. But what if, under extreme duress, it can manifest as a quantum leap? A sudden, explosive acceleration driven by collective desperation? We're seeing convergent evolution on an unprecedented scale, across thousands of species simultaneously. It's like every insect on the planet received a shared evolutionary upgrade. And we have no idea how."

Ben chimed in, frustration coloring his voice. "We've analyzed samples from dozens of different insect species. There are commonalities in the genetic markers, yes, but the specific adaptations are wildly divergent. Some have developed bioluminescent signaling, others enhanced exoskeletal plating, some exhibit an almost psionic ability to disrupt electronic frequencies. How can one singular event trigger such a diverse range of specialized responses?"

The question hung in the air, unanswered. They tried cross-referencing data from different labs, sharing their fragmented discoveries through encrypted channels, a desperate attempt to stitch together a coherent picture from a thousand shattered pieces. The consensus was grim: their understanding of biology, of evolution, of life itself, was woefully inadequate to comprehend the scale of what was happening. They were like medieval physicians trying to understand germ theory with only leeches and incantations.

"The problem," Aris stated, his voice low and grave, "is that we're still trying to find a

chemical or *genetic* explanation within our existing framework. We're looking for a virus, a pollutant, a specific trigger. But what if the trigger isn't something we can isolate in a test tube? What if it's a fundamental shift in the planet's electromagnetic field, amplified and harnessed by insectoid biology? What if their collective consciousness is, in part, a product of interacting with a planet that is itself in crisis?" The idea was bordering on the mystical, a concept that would have been laughed out of any scientific conference just weeks prior. But now, with cities falling silent and the air buzzing with a hostile, intelligent life, the boundaries between science and the inexplicable were blurring.

They analyzed the defensive strategies of the insects. The wasps, with their potent neurotoxins, seemed to target critical infrastructure, disabling communication networks and power grids with terrifying precision. The beetles, as observed in the hospital attack, demonstrated an unsettling aptitude for identifying structural weaknesses, systematically dismantling buildings as if they possessed an innate understanding of engineering. The ants, in their sheer numbers and ferocity, overwhelmed any lingering pockets of human resistance.

"It's not just about survival anymore," Lena whispered, her gaze fixed on a microscopic image of a termite's mandibles, impossibly sharp and coated with a shimmering, unknown substance. "It's about dominance. They're not just defending territory; they're actively reclaiming it."

Aris felt a cold dread seep into his bones. His life's work had been to understand and appreciate the natural world. He had advocated for conservation, for a more respectful coexistence with other species. Now, that very natural world, twisted and weaponized by humanity's own excesses, was turning on its master. The intricate web of life, which he had always seen as a delicate balance, had become a battlefield, and humanity was clearly losing.

They were running out of time. Every hour that passed brought new reports of devastation, new evidence of the insects' relentless advance. Their labs, once bastions of knowledge, were becoming mere observatories of humanity's swift and brutal decline. The scramble for answers had devolved into a desperate, often futile attempt to simply document the end, a process so profound and so alien that their scientific tools and methodologies felt laughably inadequate. They were witnesses to an evolutionary leap that had bypassed them entirely, a testament to the resilience and terrifying adaptability of life itself, a resilience born from the very ecological damage they, as a species, had inflicted. The dawn of a new biological age was upon them, an age ruled not by man, but by the ancient, newly awakened might of the insect kingdom.

The initial reports were dismissed as isolated incidents, anomalies in an increasingly chaotic world. A few rogue cicadas exhibiting unusual aggression, a swarm of locusts that seemed to deviate from their migratory patterns and attack agricultural machinery – such events were chalked up to environmental factors, perhaps a new strain of a common virus. The military, still reeling from a decade of proxy wars and simmering geopolitical tensions, viewed these entomological oddities as a low-priority concern, a nuisance rather than a threat. General Marcus Thorne, a man forged in the crucible of conventional warfare, found the notion of insects posing a significant military challenge absurd. His concern was with ballistic missiles, troop movements, and geopolitical maneuvering, not with the buzzing of flies in a mess hall. He'd seen riots quelled with greater force, rebellions stifled with fewer resources. The idea of deploying combat divisions to deal with what were essentially pests was preposterous.

However, the tide of dismissal turned with brutal swiftness. The 'isolated incidents' coalesced into a global phenomenon, a coordinated onslaught that defied all logic and expectation. The swarms grew not in numbers, but in terrifying, unified purpose. The first true alarm bells rang not in the halls of power, but in the remote outposts and garrisons where the initial skirmishes occurred. A patrol unit in the dense jungles of Southeast Asia, tasked with clearing a suspected guerrilla encampment, found itself surrounded, not by enemy combatants, but by a living, crawling tide of venomous centipedes, their segmented bodies moving with an unnerving synchronicity. The unit's heavy machine guns, designed to shred flesh and shatter fortifications, proved woefully inadequate against the sheer, unyielding mass. The creatures' chitinous armor resisted small-arms fire, and their coordinated attacks targeted exposed equipment and personnel with a precision that suggested more than mere instinct.

Across continents, similar horror stories began to filter through encrypted military channels. In the vast agricultural plains of North America, autonomous farming drones, once symbols of human ingenuity and control over the land, were systematically dismantled by gargantuan scarab beetles, their reinforced exoskeletons impervious to the drones' cutting implements. In the urban centers, legions of oversized ants, their mandibles capable of shearing through steel cables, overwhelmed early attempts at containment, their sheer numbers a biological battering ram against barricades. The chilling realization dawned: this was not a natural disaster; this was an invasion.

The military, a colossal and inherently slow-moving organism, found itself utterly unprepared. Its doctrines, honed for decades against human adversaries, were rendered obsolete overnight. The concept of 'front lines' dissolved when the enemy could emerge from the very earth beneath your feet, or descend from the sky in a suffocating cloud. Reconnaissance satellites, designed to detect troop concentrations and missile silos, were useless against a threat that was simultaneously microscopic and planetary in scale. The enemy had no discernible command structure, no supply lines to disrupt, no territorial claims to contest in the traditional sense. It was a ubiquitous foe, an omnipresent enemy woven into the very fabric of the environment.

General Thorne, his face etched with a grim new understanding, convened an emergency joint chiefs meeting. The air in the secure bunker was thick with tension, the usual pronouncements of military might replaced by a raw, desperate search for solutions. "Our conventional assets are... compromised," admitted General Davies, head of tactical operations, his voice tight with frustration. "Tanks are being immobilized by arachnid swarms that burrow beneath them, disrupting treads and cooling systems. Aircraft are struggling with swarms of metallic-winged insects capable of disrupting electronic systems and even piercing fuselage with their reinforced proboscises. We're fighting an enemy that doesn't bleed, that doesn't fear, and that seems to learn from every engagement."

The logistical challenges were immense. How does one

mobilize an army to fight an enemy that could be anywhere? Supply chains, designed to move materiel to forward operating bases, were now vulnerable to attacks from burrowing insects that could undermine roads and railways, or flying insects that could disable transport aircraft mid-flight. The sheer diversity of the threat further complicated matters. A battalion trained to combat giant centipedes was ill-equipped to deal with genetically altered wasps capable of emitting paralyzing sonic frequencies, or with colossal earthworms that could swallow armored vehicles whole.

The initial response was, predictably, brute force. Flamethrowers, relics of a bygone era of warfare, were brought out of mothballs, their streams of napalm proving effective against the sheer biomass of some insectoid assaults. But even these weapons had limitations. The sheer scale of the incursions meant that a tactical advantage gained in one sector could be lost in minutes as new swarms materialized from unexpected directions. Chemical countermeasures, developed for biological warfare against humans, were also deployed, but the insects' rapidly evolving biology meant that their efficacy was short-lived. What worked one day was rendered useless the next as the creatures adapted, developing resistances or novel defense mechanisms.

"We need to rethink our entire approach," stated Dr. Anya Sharma, a leading biochemist seconded to the military command. Her face was pale, her eyes hollowed from sleepless nights poring over captured insect specimens. "Their biology is not just resilient; it's actively adaptive. We're seeing evidence of directed evolution, of rapid gene expression changes occurring in response to our countermeasures. It's like trying to hit a moving target that's also redesigning itself as you aim."

The psychological toll on the soldiers was immense. They were trained to face human enemies, to understand their motivations, their weaknesses. This enemy was alien, its actions seemingly driven by a singular, unfathomable will. The constant, unnerving hum of a million chitinous wings, the sight of impossibly large creatures moving with terrifying coordination, the pervasive fear of the unseen—it chipped away at morale like water on stone. Soldiers reported experiencing auditory hallucinations, phantom buzzing sounds, and a constant, gnawing anxiety that they were being watched, analyzed, and judged by a collective intelligence beyond their comprehension.

General Thorne, despite his initial skepticism, now understood the gravity of the situation. He authorized the deployment of every available asset, from the most advanced drones to the humble but effective extermination units that had once been relegated to pest control. The military was no longer fighting to secure territory; it was fighting for survival. The war had moved from the traditional battlefields of nations to the very ecological niches of the planet, and humanity, for the first time in its history, found itself not as the apex predator, but as prey. The struggle was not just against a biological threat, but against a fundamental reordering of life on Earth, a reordering driven by its smallest, most overlooked inhabitants. The mobilization was not just of troops and weapons, but of a desperate, global effort to reassert dominance in a world that was rapidly, irrevocably, slipping from its grasp. Every deployed unit, every activated weapon system, was a testament to humanity's stubborn refusal to yield, even as the ground beneath them began to teem with an enemy that represented the ultimate, terrifying manifestation of nature's own desperate struggle for survival. The sheer logistics of deploying specialized units – entomological warfare specialists, bio-chemical containment teams, heavy ordnance units retrofitted to deal with armored exoskeletons – strained the global logistical network to its breaking point. Supply convoys were constantly ambushed, not by organized resistance, but by opportunistic swarms that materialized from the soil, the air, and even the waterways. The military found itself fighting a war of attrition against an enemy that suffered no casualties in the traditional sense, an enemy that seemed to replenish its ranks effortlessly from the very planet it was reclaiming. The concept of 'victory' itself began to warp; survival became the only metric that mattered.

The echoes of the past, once a distant whisper, now roared in the ears of a humbled humanity. The sheer, unadulterated terror of the ongoing entomological onslaught had a way of stripping away the veneer of progress, exposing the raw, exposed nerves of collective guilt. For decades, humanity had acted as a planetary sovereign, issuing decrees of chemical dominion over the natural world. The fields, once vibrant with the cacophony of native life, had been sterilized, transformed into monocultures amenable to efficient, industrialized agriculture. The ubiquitous hum of insects, once a constant backdrop to life, had been systematically silenced by a relentless barrage of pesticides, herbicides, and insecticides. These weren't just chemicals; they were pronouncements of war against any life that dared to exist outside of human design and control.

This war, waged with a casual, almost thoughtless brutality, had been fought on a billion fronts, across every continent, in every ecosystem. The objective was simple: maximize yield, minimize perceived pests, and profit. The long-term consequences, the intricate web of life that supported these very crops, were a secondary, often ignored, consideration. Entomologists, those few who still dedicated their lives to the study of insects, had warned of the dangers. They spoke of the essential roles pollinators played, the natural pest control provided by predatory insects, the vital decomposition services performed by countless smaller creatures. Their voices, however, were often drowned out by the booming pronouncements of chemical companies and the relentless pursuit of greater agricultural output. The warnings were dismissed as alarmist, the science inconvenient, the messengers irrelevant in the face of profit margins and feeding a growing global population.

Now, the irony was as bitter as it was undeniable. The very creatures that had been systematically targeted, hunted, and eradicated with every chemical weapon humanity could devise, had not only survived but had seemingly evolved, mutated, and organized into a force that threatened to consume its former oppressor. The colossal scarab beetles, their exoskeletons now capable of shrugging off the reinforced plating of autonomous harvesters, were the descendants of humble dung beetles, their populations decimated by broad-spectrum insecticides that killed indiscriminately. The venomous centipedes, capable of overwhelming armored patrols, likely originated from species driven to the brink of extinction by habitat destruction and targeted extermination campaigns. Even the monstrous ants, now capable of breaching steel, were warped iterations of insects once easily subdued by a sprinkle of borax.

A profound, gnawing sense of responsibility began to settle upon those who could still think, who could still reason amidst the chaos. It wasn't just a matter of external aggression; it was an indictment. In the secure, fortified bunkers, where the remnants of human command attempted to coordinate a defense, hushed conversations turned to this uncomfortable truth. Dr. Aris Thorne, the younger brother of General Thorne and a renowned ecologist who had been marginalized for his outspoken critiques of agricultural policy, found himself in a unique, albeit terrifying, position. His past research, once dismissed as irrelevant, now served as a grim roadmap to understanding the enemy.

"We treated the planet like a canvas for our own ambitions," Aris explained to a group of bewildered military strategists, his voice hoarse, his face etched with a weariness that transcended mere lack of sleep. "We eradicated species with the same ease that we swat a fly. We poured poisons into the soil, the water, the air, believing we were masters of our domain, impervious to the repercussions. We created an ecological vacuum, and into that vacuum, something far more resilient, far more unified, has stepped."

He gestured to the holographic displays, now dominated by the swirling masses of insectoid threats. "Look at their behavior. It's not random. It's... strategic. They are exploiting the weaknesses we created. They are reclaiming territories we rendered sterile. The very genetic engineering we used to enhance our crops, to create drought-resistant strains, to improve nutritional value – it seems they have intercepted and amplified that knowledge. Or perhaps, in their desperation to survive our chemical onslaught, they developed their own rapid, directed evolution. We pushed them, and they pushed back, not with reason or malice as we understand it, but with the unyielding imperative of existence."

The weight of this realization was crushing. It wasn't just the battlefield that was lost; it was the moral high ground, the narrative of human superiority. The war wasn't a fight against an alien invader from the stars, but against the consequences of humanity's own destructive tendencies, amplified and weaponized by nature itself. The sheer hubris of believing that life could be so easily controlled, so casually annihilated, was now the most potent weapon in the enemy's arsenal.

Aris recounted his personal experiences, the chilling moments of foresight that had been ignored. "I remember a study, years ago, on the effects of neonicotinoids on bee populations. We saw the colony collapse, the disorientation, the death. But we focused on the economic impact, on finding alternative pollinators, on developing even stronger pesticides to combat the pests that the dying bees could no longer control. We never considered the possibility that these chemicals, designed to disrupt insect nervous systems, might have unintended consequences on a grander scale. What if they were inadvertently *rewiring* them? What if they were, in their own alien way, learning to weaponize our own poisons against us?"

The implications sent a shiver through the room. If the insects were indeed adapting to the very chemicals humanity had used to subjugate them, then every countermeasure, every attempt at chemical warfare, was a gamble. It was a terrifying game of biological chess where the opponent learned from every move, evolving faster than human ingenuity could adapt. The concept of a 'kill switch' for this infestation, once a confident military objective, now seemed laughably naive.

The guilt manifested in different ways. Some men and women in positions of power, those who had signed off on the widespread use of these chemicals, now withdrew into themselves, their faces gaunt, their eyes avoiding contact. Others, like General Thorne, channeled their burgeoning guilt into a furious, desperate resolve to fight, to protect the remaining pockets of humanity, even if they knew the fight was born from their own past transgressions. There were also those who, in their terror and despair, sought to assign blame elsewhere – to foreign powers, to rogue scientists, to anything but their own collective species. But the evidence was too stark, too overwhelming. The scarred landscapes, the depleted biodiversity, the ghost towns of once-thriving agricultural communities – they all bore witness to humanity's environmental recklessness.

"We need to understand their motivations," Aris insisted, his voice gaining an urgency that cut through the despair. "Not as humans understand motivation, but as a biological imperative. They are not driven by conquest for conquest's sake, but by survival. By the instinct to propagate, to reclaim their place. Our cities, our infrastructure, our very way of life – to them, these are just obstacles, disruptions in the natural order. And the chemicals we used, the genetic modifications we introduced into our crops, the sterile environments we created... these were not defenses; they were provocateurs."

The sheer scale of the problem was a stark reminder of the interconnectedness of all living things. Humanity, in its arrogance, had attempted to isolate itself from the natural world, to control it, to bend it to its will. But nature, as it turned out, was a vast, complex, and interconnected system, and tampering with its fundamental building blocks had unleashed forces that were now beyond human comprehension or control. The cost of ignorance, the price of ecological negligence, was being paid in blood, in terror, and in the existential threat of extinction. The war wasn't just against giant insects; it was a reckoning with the consequences of centuries of ecological disregard, a brutal lesson delivered by the very life that humanity had so carelessly tried to extinguish. The silence that followed Aris's pronouncements was heavy, pregnant with the unspoken admission that the enemy at the gates was, in a horrifyingly literal sense, a reflection of humanity's own destructive nature. The question was no longer whether humanity could win, but whether it deserved to.

A New Dawn

SHIFTING TIDES

The initial human response, a crude but brutal application of overwhelming force, had been met with a tide of chitin and venom. Now, the vast insectoid coalition, a nascent global consciousness born from shared persecution, was not merely reacting; it was strategizing. The chaotic swarms that had initially overwhelmed isolated outposts were evolving, their movements becoming more coordinated, their assaults more calculated. This was not the mindless aggression of individual creatures driven by instinct alone, but the emergent intelligence of a species – or rather, a multitude of species – fighting a war for its very existence.

Aris Thorne, his early pronouncements of ecological consequence now chillingly validated, found himself at the forefront of deciphering this evolving threat. His team, a motley collection of surviving entomologists, biologists, and even disillusioned agricultural scientists, worked feverishly within the sterile confines of the bunker, piecing together the fragmented intelligence reports. "They're not just attacking; they're *adapting*," Aris explained, his voice raspy from lack of sleep and the ever-present dust that seemed to seep through even the most robust filtration systems. He gestured to a complex, three-dimensional map that pulsed with the activity of the insect legions. "The initial wave was a brute-force assault, overwhelming our defenses through sheer numbers and shock value. But the engagements since then... they show a distinct learning curve."

One of the most significant developments was the

emergence of sophisticated communication methods. Gone were the days of purely pheromonal signaling, adequate for localized colonies but insufficient for a planetary-scale alliance. The evidence suggested a multi-modal communication network, leveraging a combination of bio-luminescence, infrasonic vibrations, and even subtle shifts in atmospheric ionization. Dr. Lena Hanson, a former researcher in bio-acoustics, had been instrumental in identifying these subtle patterns. "We're detecting complex vibrational sequences emanating from the larger insectoid command units, the 'nexus points' as we've started calling them," she reported, her eyes fixed on a series of oscillating wave patterns on her monitor. "These aren't random; they're highly structured, almost like a highly compressed data stream. They seem to be coordinating movements across vast distances, relaying battlefield intelligence, and even... sharing environmental data."

This environmental data sharing was particularly concerning. The insects were no longer just reacting to human presence; they were actively manipulating their surroundings. Reports from recon drones, though increasingly scarce and unreliable, indicated instances of massive termite colonies constructing complex subterranean networks, not merely for shelter, but as conduits for rapid troop deployment and the redistribution of resources. In arid regions, nomadic locust swarms were observed congregating around specific atmospheric pressure fronts, seemingly triggering localized microbursts of moisture to encourage vegetation growth in their wake – a chillingly effective form of terraforming.

"It's as if they've absorbed our own agricultural knowledge, twisted it, and turned it back on us," mused Dr. Jian Li, a geneticist whose work on drought-resistant crops had once been hailed as revolutionary, now a source of profound regret. "The sheer efficiency with which they're utilizing resources, the speed at which they're colonizing and adapting to previously inhospitable environments... it's biological engineering on an unprecedented scale. We theorized about directed evolution, about accelerating natural selection. It seems they've achieved it, not through conscious intent as we understand it, but through the relentless pressure of our own actions."

The insect alliance had also developed new defensive capabilities. The colossal scarab beetles, once vulnerable to sustained kinetic impact, were now observed emitting localized sonic pulses capable of disrupting the targeting systems of armored vehicles. This was not a chemical weapon, but a bio-mechanical one, an adaptation born from exposure to the very sonic deterrents humans had deployed in an attempt to disorient them. Similarly, centipede swarms were now employing a unique form of chemical warfare. Instead of relying solely on their natural venom, they were observed secreting a viscous, corrosive fluid, derived from processed fungal spores found in the ruins of abandoned chemical plants. This fluid was highly effective at degrading metal alloys, turning tanks and APCs into rusting hulks within hours.

"The fungal spores," Aris elaborated, pointing to a microscopic analysis of the fluid. "They're not just secreting it; they're actively cultivating and processing it. This implies a level of metabolic specialization and resource management we hadn't anticipated. It's like they've unlocked the secrets of our own industrial chemical production, but through biological means."

Offensively, the strategies were becoming even more audacious. The ant legions, those terrifying, steel-breaching monstrosities, were no longer content with simply dismantling fortifications. They had begun to utilize their immense numbers and relentless digging capabilities to create sophisticated tunnel systems that bypassed conventional defenses entirely. In urban environments, these ant-built tunnels acted as arterial networks, allowing for surprise attacks from beneath ground level, collapsing buildings from their foundations and creating chaotic breaches for other insectoid units to exploit. There were even anecdotal reports, still largely unconfirmed due to the sheer danger involved, of certain ant species developing the ability to secrete a rapidly hardening resin, effectively encasing human strongholds and personnel in an impenetrable, suffocating tomb.

The airborne threat had also evolved. The gargantuan moths, once primarily a nuisance due to their sheer size and disorienting dust clouds, had now become strategic assets. They were observed carrying and dispersing massive quantities of parasitic spores, targeting not only human settlements but also the remaining livestock and even hardy vegetation that humanity relied upon for sustenance. Furthermore, some species of large predatory wasps were now exhibiting an uncanny ability to track heat signatures and electromagnetic emissions, making even the most sophisticated stealth technology obsolete. Their attacks were no longer opportunistic raids; they were precision strikes, guided by an intelligence that seemed to anticipate human movements.

"Their communication isn't just about coordination; it's about shared knowledge," Aris stated, his gaze distant, lost in the terrifying implications. "Imagine a billion individual insects, each with a slightly different sensory input, a slightly different environmental experience. Now imagine that data being fed into a collective network, analyzed, and integrated. They're learning from every skirmish, every failed human tactic. They're building a comprehensive operational understanding of our strengths and weaknesses, and they're exploiting every single one."

The concept of 'terrain' had also taken on a new meaning for the insect alliance. They were not merely inhabiting the landscape; they were actively reshaping it to their advantage. In areas previously rendered toxic by human industrial activity, hardy, genetically resilient fungi and bacteria, long dormant or struggling to survive, were now being actively cultivated by specialized insectoid species. These organisms, in turn, provided camouflage, sustenance, and even new chemical defenses that further hampered human efforts to reclaim territory. The ruined cities, symbols of humanity's hubris, were becoming blooming gardens of bio-engineered horror, their very decay feeding the engine of the new world order.

General Thorne, Aris's elder brother, a man forged in the crucible of conventional warfare, struggled to grasp the fluid, organic nature of this new enemy. His mind was trained for front lines, for fortified positions, for quantifiable objectives. This was an amorphous, adaptive threat that seemed to learn and evolve in real-time. "They are a distributed network," Aris had explained to him, using terms more familiar to military command. "There is no single command center to decapitate, no single leader to assassinate. The 'leadership' is inherent in the network itself, in the collective intelligence that flows through it."

The sheer variety of species involved, once a point of human scientific fascination, was now the source of their terrifying advantage. A single ant colony might be easily repelled, but an alliance that included the burrowing capabilities of termites, the aerial assault of moths, the venomous strikes of centipedes, and the brute force of scarabs presented a multifaceted challenge that no single human doctrine could adequately address. They were a symphony of destruction, each species playing its part in a grand, terrifying opera of planetary reclamation.

Aris projected images of insect nests that had been discovered, not the simple mounds and burrows of pre-apocalypse times, but vast, intricate complexes, often partially integrated with surviving human structures. These were not just living spaces; they were operational hubs, research and development centers, and logistical nightmares for any human force attempting to dislodge them. "Look at this," he said, zooming in on a segment of a massive, pulsating hive discovered beneath the ruins of a former research facility. "These structures incorporate salvaged electronic components, rudimentary bio-electric generators, and what appear to be chemical synthesis vats, all organically integrated. They are not simply using our abandoned technology; they are *becoming* it, integrating it into their own biological framework."

The implications of this integration were staggering. It suggested that the insects were not only adapting to existing human threats but were actively seeking out and repurposing human technological advancements for their own purposes. The war had become a desperate struggle for survival, where the very tools humanity had used to assert its dominance were being systematically co-opted and weaponized against it. The tide had not just shifted; it had fundamentally transformed into a new and terrifying paradigm, one where the battlefield was no longer defined by geography, but by the relentless, evolving strategies of a planet's reawakened, and furious, indigenous life. Humanity was no longer the predator; it was the prey, and its former prey was now orchestrating a global campaign with a chilling, alien precision. The nest of strategies was vast, interconnected, and growing more sophisticated with every passing, blood-soaked hour.

The earth itself had become a battlefield, a vast, churning maw that swallowed human defenses from below. The ant legions, those colossal, six-legged titans of destruction, had perfected the art of subterranean warfare. Their tunnels, once mere pathways for colony expansion, were now meticulously engineered arteries of invasion, precisely mapped and strategically deployed to cripple humanity's remaining infrastructure. Foundations of fortified bunkers, once considered impregnable, were now meticulously undermined, their weight a constant, terrifying pressure against the chitinous claws that gnawed at their support structures.

These were not the haphazard tunnels of mindless burrowing. The ants, in their terrifying new collective consciousness, had learned to identify structural weak points, to sense the subtle shifts in stress within concrete and steel. They moved with an unsettling synchronicity, a biological demolition crew working with terrifying efficiency. Reports from the dwindling network of seismic sensors painted a grim picture: a constant hum of activity beneath the surface, a silent tremor that spoke of relentless excavation. Each tremor was a potential collapse, each seismic anomaly a harbinger of destruction to come.

The ant species involved were not monolithic. Some, like the 'Breachers,' were massive, almost ox-like in their proportions, their mandibles capable of shearing through rebar and reinforced concrete with chilling ease. Then there were the 'Miners,' smaller but infinitely more numerous, their specialized forelimbs designed for rapid soil displacement and tunnel reinforcement, ensuring the structural integrity of their underground campaigns. They worked in shifts, a ceaseless, organic tide of destruction, pushing deeper into the earth, inch by agonizing inch, towards the vital arteries of human survival.

Utility lines, the very lifelines of the beleaguered human resistance, were prime targets. Water mains, buried deep for protection, were systematically breached, their precious contents flooding lower levels, creating treacherous, disorienting conditions. Power conduits, the arteries carrying the last vestiges of electricity, were severed, plunging vital installations into darkness and crippling communication arrays. The insects seemed to possess an innate understanding of these systems, their actions driven by a primal, yet disturbingly informed, logic. They understood that by severing these connections, they could isolate and starve the human strongholds, turning them into tomb-like prisons.

Transportation networks, already ravaged by surface-level assaults, now faced a new threat from beneath. Subway tunnels, remnants of a bygone era of mass transit, were being systematically collapsed, the sheer volume of displaced earth and debris blocking escape routes and cutting off vital supply lines. In some cases, the ants had repurposed these subterranean arteries, transforming them into highways for their own legions, allowing them to bypass surface defenses and emerge unexpectedly in the heart of human-occupied zones. These were not simply conquered territories; they were being actively re-engineered, reshaped to serve the needs of the new, chitinous masters.

The sheer scale of the underground operations was almost incomprehensible. Vast networks of tunnels, interconnected and spanning miles, were being constructed with a speed and precision that defied human understanding. Specialized fungal growths, cultivated by certain ant species, were used to reinforce tunnel walls, secreting a hardened, resin-like substance that made their creations incredibly resilient. These bio-engineered reinforcements also served a secondary purpose: they exuded a subtle, yet potent, bio-luminescent glow, providing their subterranean armies with a dim, eerie light source, while simultaneously blinding any human sensor systems attempting to penetrate the darkness.

The earth itself had become a weapon in their arsenal. Instead of relying solely on their physical might, the insects learned to weaponize the very ground they moved through. Controlled collapses were orchestrated, triggered by precise vibrations or the release of specialized chemical agents that destabilized the soil. These cave-ins were not random acts of destruction; they were carefully timed diversions, or devastating traps, designed to disorient and incapacitate human response teams attempting to counter their subterranean incursions. Imagine a squad of soldiers, painstakingly clearing a tunnel, only for the very ground beneath their feet to erupt, sending them tumbling into an abyss of churning earth and venomous mandibles.

The intelligence gathering on the human side was a desperate, ongoing struggle. Every seismic spike, every anomalous ground vibration, was analyzed with feverish intensity. Dr. Aris Thorne and his team worked tirelessly, trying to predict the next devastating thrust of the ant legions, to anticipate where the next foundation would crumble, where the next vital conduit would be severed. They cross-referenced geological surveys with known ant colony expansion patterns, attempting to find some semblance of predictability in the chaos.

"It's not just about digging anymore," Lena Hanson, her face etched with exhaustion, explained during a particularly tense briefing. "They're creating pressure differentials. They're manipulating groundwater levels. We've detected localized seismic activity that doesn't correspond to typical burrowing patterns. It's almost as if they're creating controlled tremors to destabilize larger structures, a kind of bio-engineered demolition charge."

The implications were terrifying. The insects weren't just attacking; they were actively studying and exploiting the vulnerabilities of human engineering, using their innate connection to the earth to dismantle the very foundations of human civilization. The war was no longer fought solely on the surface, under the open sky. A new front had opened, a silent, insidious war waged in the perpetual darkness beneath the ravaged landscapes, a war that threatened to consume humanity from its very roots.

The human resistance, largely confined to scattered bunkers and fortified underground facilities, found themselves increasingly vulnerable to this unseen enemy. The constant threat of collapse, the insidious undermining of their defenses, the disruption of essential services – it was a war of attrition waged on a geological scale. The earth, once a symbol of stability and resilience, had become a treacherous accomplice to their insectoid adversaries.

In the abandoned transit systems, the ants carved their own cities, vast, interconnected metropolises hidden from the surface world. These were not mere nests; they were breeding grounds, logistical hubs, and strategic planning centers, all interwoven with the earth itself. Luminescent fungi pulsed with an alien light, illuminating vast chambers where new generations of soldier ants were nurtured, their mandibles already sharp, their instincts honed for destruction.

The sound of their relentless activity, though often masked by the ambient groans of collapsing structures or the distant roars of surface battles, was a constant, subliminal reminder of their presence. It was the sound of ceaseless digging, of chitin scraping against rock, of millions of tiny feet moving in unison. It was the sound of the earth being rewritten, of a new order being forged in the darkness.

The human efforts to counter this subterranean menace were often heroic, but ultimately, they felt like fighting ghosts. Deploying seismic charges to collapse tunnels often triggered larger, more devastating chain reactions, destabilizing wider areas and endangering their own positions. Attempts to flood tunnels were met with specialized ant species that could seal breaches with remarkable speed or simply reroute their entire operations to drier, unaffected sectors. It was a constant game of cat and mouse, played out in the suffocating darkness, where every advantage gained by humanity was invariably countered by an even more ingenious adaptation from their insectoid foes.

The sheer willpower of the ant legions was a force to be reckoned with. There was no fatigue, no dissent, only a collective drive to dismantle, to destroy, to reclaim. They would labor for days, for weeks, on a single objective – the undermining of a critical support pillar, the breaching of a vital water pipe – their unwavering focus a terrifying testament to their emergent intelligence. The earth itself seemed to whisper their intentions, a low rumble that sent shivers down the spines of the bunker dwellers. This was the slow, inexorable advance of a new age, an age where humanity's dominion was being systematically eroded, not from above, but from the very depths of the planet. The ground beneath their feet was no longer a foundation; it was a grave.

The earth, once humanity's unwavering foundation, had become a treacherous enemy, its depths echoing with the ceaseless, insidious work of the ant legions. But as the ground churned and buckled, a different kind of dread began to creep in, a chilling awareness that the war for survival was no longer confined to the subterranean realm. The skies, once a boundless expanse of freedom, were rapidly becoming a new battleground, one where the enemy moved with a swiftness and ferocity that defied conventional understanding. The aerial dominance of the insectoid forces was not a mere strategic advantage; it was a declaration of total environmental control, a pervasive threat that tightened the noose around humanity's dwindling sanctuary.

The arrival of the killer bees and their colossal wasp counterparts marked a terrifying evolution in the insectoid war machine. These were not the simple pests of memory, easily swatted away or deterred. Evolution, accelerated by the same emergent consciousness that guided the subterranean legions, had transformed them into apex predators of the air. Their flight patterns, once erratic and instinctual, were now meticulously coordinated, a mesmerizing, terrifying ballet of death. Swarms of bees, numbering in the tens of thousands, could coalesce in an instant, forming living, breathing aerial fortresses. Their buzzing, a low, ominous hum that carried on the wind, was no longer a distant annoyance but a constant, unnerving reminder of their omnipresent gaze.

The initial human response was to rely on their own aerial assets – modified drones, salvaged VTOL aircraft, and the few remaining fighter jets that had escaped the initial onslaught. These were sorties of desperation, attempts to reassert control over the airspace, to reclaim the freedom of movement that was so vital to their survival. But the insectoid air forces were prepared. They had learned, adapted, and, most chillingly, innovated.

The killer bees, with their incredibly sensitive olfactory receptors, could track the exhaust trails of aircraft for miles, their approach a silent, deadly pursuit. They had developed an uncanny ability to identify and exploit weaknesses in human aerial technology. Their initial attacks were often focused on sensor arrays and exposed control surfaces, areas where a few well-placed stings, laced with a potent neurotoxin, could disable an entire aircraft. The sheer density of a bee swarm could overwhelm even the most advanced countermeasures. Sonic deterrents, once effective, were now drowned out by the cacophony of a million wings beating in unison. Flares, designed to decoy heat-seeking missiles, were simply ignored, the insects' internal thermal regulation far exceeding the primitive capabilities of human weaponry.

The wasps, larger and more heavily armored, played a different, yet equally devastating role. Their chitinous exoskeletons, hardened by evolutionary pressures, could withstand small-arms fire, and their powerful mandibles could rip through the fuselage of smaller aircraft. They acted as shock troops, spearheading assaults, their sheer mass and aggression enough to shatter defensive formations. They had also discovered a terrifying new tactic: weaponizing the very weather.

During particularly violent thunderstorms, the wasps seemed to revel in the chaos. They would hover near the electrical discharges, their bodies absorbing and amplifying the static electricity. Then, in a terrifying display of bio-engineering, they would discharge this stored energy in focused bursts, akin to living tasers, capable of frying aircraft electronics or incapacitating pilots even within shielded cockpits. Survivors of these encounters spoke of streaks of blinding light, of aircraft spiraling uncontrollably from the sky, engulfed in crackling arcs of emerald energy.

The winds, too, became an ally of the insectoid aerial forces. During high winds, while human aircraft struggled for stability, the bees and wasps, with their superior maneuverability and finely tuned wingspans, could navigate the turbulent air with alarming ease. They used the strong gusts to propel themselves at incredible speeds, ambushing human craft from unexpected angles. It was as if the very atmosphere had been re-written to favor their aerial dominance, every gust of wind a potential weapon, every cloud a temporary sanctuary for their unseen maneuvers.

The psychological impact of this aerial onslaught was profound. The constant, low hum of the approaching swarms was a pervasive dread, a sound that could reduce even the most hardened soldier to a state of anxious vigilance. The sight of a vast, dark cloud blotting out the sun, coalescing from the horizon, was a harbinger of impending doom. There was no longer any safe haven, no sky to escape to, only a vast, indifferent expanse that now served as the hunting ground for humanity's most formidable foe.

Dr. Aris Thorne and his team at the underground research facility found themselves scrambling to understand the full extent of this aerial threat. Their seismic sensors, so crucial in tracking the subterranean ant legions, were useless against an enemy that moved through the air. They relied on visual confirmation, on radar sweeps that were increasingly unreliable due to the sheer density of insectoid formations and their ability to jam or disrupt human tracking systems.

"It's a complete paradigm shift," Lena Hanson stated during one particularly grim briefing, her voice strained. "Our entire defense strategy was based on ground-based infrastructure and limited air support. They've effectively neutralized our mobility and our ability to scout and resupply. They are not just attacking us; they are isolating us."

The data coming in was fragmented and terrifying. Reports detailed swarms of bees overwhelming ground-based anti-air emplacements, their sheer numbers and relentless attacks proving too much for even the most robust defenses. Wasps were observed dive-bombing reconnaissance vehicles, their impact shattering the armored glass and neutralizing the occupants. The insects seemed to coordinate their attacks with an almost unnerving precision, overwhelming key defensive points with coordinated bee assaults while wasps provided heavy artillery support, smashing through fortifications that had previously been considered impenetrable.

The concept of "aerial superiority" was becoming a cruel jest. For humanity, it was a distant memory, a relic of a time when the sky was theirs to command. For the insectoid forces, it was a tangible, terrifying reality they were actively enforcing. They patrolled the skies with an unyielding presence, their movements dictated by a collective will that left no room for error or hesitation. Every flight path, every reconnaissance mission undertaken by humans, was met with swift and brutal retaliation.

The strategic implications were dire. Without air superiority, humanity was effectively grounded. Supply lines, already precarious due to the subterranean ant legions, were now completely severed. Any attempt to move personnel or resources between scattered strongholds was a suicide mission, the skies a minefield of buzzing death. Communication networks, reliant on airborne relays and drone footage, were constantly under attack, leaving pockets of survivors isolated and unaware of the true scope of the unfolding catastrophe.

The insects' ability to weaponize natural phenomena was particularly alarming. The deliberate manipulation of static electricity during storms was a terrifying advancement, suggesting a level of understanding of atmospheric physics that was both shocking and deeply unsettling. Scientists speculated that the wasps might possess specialized organs capable of accumulating and discharging electrical energy, a product of their accelerated evolution. The implications were staggering: if they could control the very elements, what other natural forces could they bend to their will?

Consider the case of the remnants of the Aurora base, a once-thriving research facility nestled in a remote mountain range. Their last desperate attempt to establish an aerial bridge for critical supplies was met with an unprecedented assault. A massive swarm of killer bees, estimated to be over a million strong, converged on their lone cargo VTOL. Simultaneously, a squadron of giant wasps, their bodies shimmering with an eerie phosphorescence, began to deliberately disrupt the local atmospheric conditions.

As the VTOL ascended, a sudden, localized downdraft, unnaturally powerful, slammed it back towards the earth. Before the pilots could regain control, the bee swarm enveloped the aircraft. The thrumming intensified, vibrating through the metal hull like a death knell. Then, arcs of blue-white energy, emanating from the wasps hovering at the periphery of the swarm, lanced out, striking the VTOL's engines. Sparks flew, control surfaces seized, and the aircraft plummeted, disintegrating into a fiery inferno before it even cleared the base perimeter. The few who witnessed it from the ground described it as a controlled demolition, orchestrated by nature's most terrifying architects.

This event was not an anomaly. Similar incidents were being reported across the globe, each one a testament to the insectoids' growing mastery of the skies. Their swarm tactics were evolving beyond simple numbers; they were developing coordinated attack vectors, using the wasps as heavy bombers and the bees as precision strike units. They would feign a frontal assault, drawing human defenses out, only to have flanking swarms emerge from unexpected directions, their attacks timed with chilling accuracy.

The constant surveillance from above created an inescapable sense of vulnerability. Every shadow cast by a passing cloud, every distant buzz of wings, was a source of intense anxiety. The very concept of an open sky was a bitter irony. It was no longer a symbol of hope, but a constant, oppressive presence, a reminder that humanity was being watched, judged, and systematically hunted from a vantage point it could no longer contest. The world had become a cage, and the bars were made of buzzing wings and chitinous armor, extending as far as the eye could see, stretching into every corner of the once-familiar horizon. The tide had indeed shifted, not just on the ground, but in the very air that sustained life.

The silence that had once been a comfort was now a deafening absence, a void filled only by the gnawing realization of human impotence. The initial, desperate attempts to fight back in the skies had proven catastrophically insufficient. The sophisticated drone swarms, once a symbol of humanity's technological prowess, were now mere gnats against the relentless aerial tide. Fighter jets, relics of a bygone era of dominance, were quickly swatted from the sky, their advanced avionics no match for the insects' innate, terrifying adaptations. The very air, once humanity's dominion, had become a suffocating blanket of buzzing death, each wingbeat a hammer blow against the fragile edifice of civilization.

Yet, the human spirit, forged in the crucible of countless survival struggles, refused to break. In the face of overwhelming odds, desperation bred innovation, and the scattered remnants of humanity began to cobble together countermeasures, each one a gamble, each one a testament to their unyielding will to endure. The research facilities, burrowed deep within the earth, became feverish hives of frantic scientific endeavor. Dr. Aris Thorne and his team, their faces etched with exhaustion and a grim determination, poured over fragmented data, searching for any sliver of weakness, any vulnerability in the insectoid war machine that had so swiftly and brutally seized control of the skies.

One of the first, most ambitious undertakings was the re-purposing of industrial-scale pest control technologies. Entire cities, or what remained of them, became testing grounds for massive fumigation efforts. Gigantic, modified agricultural sprayers, once used to blanket fields in pesticides, were repurposed to churn out vast quantities of newly developed chemical agents. These were not the broad-spectrum toxins of the past, designed to kill any living thing. Instead, the scientists focused on targeted bio-agents, synthesized to exploit specific biochemical pathways unique to the insectoid species. Early trials involved airborne dispersal units, essentially heavily armored cargo planes retrofitted with massive spray tanks. These lumbering behemoths, escorted by the last vestiges of aerial defense, would attempt to blanket suspected insectoid congregation zones – colossal nests clinging to the skeletons of skyscrapers or vast, buzzing formations that darkened the horizon.

The results were a mixed, often devastating, bag. Some agents proved remarkably effective, causing rapid cellular breakdown and incapacitation in the target insects. A particularly potent concoction, dubbed "Chitin-Dissolve," managed to weaken the insects' exoskeletons, making them brittle and prone to fragmentation in flight. However, the sheer scale of the insectoid population meant that such localized successes were often overwhelmed. The chemicals, while potent, were also volatile and difficult to deploy with the precision required. Unpredictable wind currents, often exacerbated by the insects' own aerial maneuvers, would scatter the agent, rendering it useless or, in some terrifying instances, concentrating its effects on human settlements instead of their intended targets.

Furthermore, the insects themselves proved remarkably adaptable. Within weeks of widespread deployment, reports began to emerge of resistance developing. Certain colonies, through sheer biological luck or accelerated evolutionary adaptation, seemed to exhibit a natural immunity to specific agents. This necessitated a constant, desperate race to develop new formulations, a game of cat and mouse where humanity was perpetually one step behind. The ethical implications also weighed heavily on the scientists. The potential for these potent chemicals to contaminate water sources, render arable land toxic for generations, or even cause unintended mutations in surviving flora and fauna, was a chilling prospect. The very weapons they were developing to save humanity could also irrevocably damage the planet they were fighting to reclaim.

Another avenue of research focused on sonic countermeasures. Building on decades of limited research into acoustic pest deterrents, scientists worked to develop high-frequency emitters capable of disrupting the insects' sensory organs and communication networks. These devices were designed to generate sonic waves so intense and at such specific frequencies that they would cause debilitating pain and disorientation to the insects. The theory was that a sustained sonic barrage could create no-fly zones, forcing the insectoid forces to retreat or, at the very least, disrupting their coordinated attacks.

The initial deployments of these sonic projectors were met with cautious optimism. Mobile units, mounted on heavily armored ground vehicles or even repurposed naval vessels, were strategically positioned around critical human enclaves. When activated, the results were sometimes dramatic. Swarms would visibly recoil, their formations breaking as individual insects thrashed erratically, seemingly overwhelmed by the invisible onslaught. However, like the chemical agents, the sonic repellents had limitations. The range was often disappointing, requiring a dense network of emitters to achieve any significant effect. Moreover, the insects quickly learned to mitigate the effects. Some colonies began to adapt by developing thicker ear coverings or by migrating to higher altitudes where the sonic waves dissipated more rapidly. The most disturbing development was the discovery that certain insectoid species, particularly the larger wasps, seemed to be able to emit counter-frequencies, effectively jamming human sonic weaponry or even turning the sonic attacks back on the operators.

The ethical quandary surrounding sonic weapons was less pronounced than that of chemical agents, but the potential for unintended consequences remained. The intense sonic vibrations could cause structural damage to human infrastructure and even induce physical distress in human personnel exposed for prolonged periods. Whispers circulated within the research facilities of a sonic frequency so potent, so precisely tuned to the insects' neural architecture, that it was theorized to be lethal. The development of such a weapon, however, was fraught with peril, raising specters of mass extinction events and the irreversible alteration of the planet's acoustic landscape.

Beyond the more conventional, albeit escalated, approaches, humanity's desperation led them down darker, more experimental paths. One such endeavor involved the creation of biological agents designed to specifically target the emergent consciousness guiding the insectoid legions. The prevailing theory was that the rapid evolution and unprecedented coordination of the insectoid forces were driven by a centralized, or at least highly interconnected, form of intelligence. If this intelligence could be disrupted or corrupted, it might cripple the entire insectoid war machine.

This led to the development of what the scientists grimly referred to as "Cognitive Contaminants." These were not simple viruses or bacteria, but rather complex, genetically engineered nanobots and retroviruses designed to infiltrate the insects' nervous systems and interfere with their collective intelligence. The initial concept involved releasing these agents into known insectoid nesting sites or along their major aerial transit routes. The hope was that the contagion would spread through the interconnectedness of the insectoid hive mind, sowing confusion, disabling coordinated attacks, and ultimately leading to a collapse of their organized resistance.

The early trials were conducted in heavily secured, isolated environments, using captured specimens. The results were initially promising, if terrifying. Insects exposed to the cognitive contaminants exhibited erratic behavior, their movements becoming uncoordinated and their aggression devolving into confused thrashing. Some specimens became catatonic, while others attacked anything in sight, including members of their own species. However, the challenges of deployment were immense. The sheer scale of the insectoid populations made it nearly impossible to achieve the critical mass of infection required for systemic collapse. Moreover, the insects' rapid evolutionary capacity meant that resistance could emerge with alarming speed. The nanobots themselves were prone to degradation in the environment, and the viruses, while potent, could also mutate into less effective or even inert forms.

The ethical precipice humanity stood upon with these cognitive contaminants was precipitous. The potential for these agents to cause widespread neurological damage, not just to the targeted insects but to any complex biological system, was a terrifying unknown. There were fears that such agents, if they escaped containment, could spread to other animal populations, causing unpredictable and potentially catastrophic ecological consequences. The very idea of intentionally weaponizing the fundamental mechanisms of consciousness, even in a non-human species, felt like a transgression, a step into a moral void from which there might be no return.

Amidst these large-scale, often fraught, countermeasure efforts, individual acts of defiance and ingenious improvisation became the lifeblood of human survival. Small, highly mobile units, equipped with specialized weaponry, began to engage in hit-and-run tactics against insectoid patrols. These were often former military personnel, pilots, and engineers who had managed to salvage and adapt whatever technology they could find. They repurposed vehicle-mounted laser systems, turning them into crude but effective anti-air defenses. Improvised electromagnetic pulse (EMP) devices, designed to disrupt insectoid flight controls or sensory arrays, were deployed with varying degrees of success.

One notable example was the "Whisper Net," a desperate attempt to create a localized, covert communication network shielded from insectoid surveillance and jamming. Using low-frequency radio waves and encrypted burst transmissions, small pockets of survivors could maintain contact, coordinate movements, and share vital intelligence. This required constant movement and an intimate understanding of the terrain, as any fixed antenna or prolonged transmission would draw the attention of the ever-vigilant aerial predators.

The scarcity of resources became a constant, gnawing problem. Every bullet, every drop of fuel, every functioning piece of technology was a precious commodity. Scavenging missions into abandoned cities became increasingly perilous, with survivors having to contend not only with the lingering insectoid threat but also with the structural instability of the ruined metropolises and the pervasive dangers of contaminated environments. Yet, these missions also yielded unexpected discoveries. Modified flamethrowers, originally designed for urban pacification, were found to be surprisingly effective against swarms of smaller insects. Modified sonic emitters, repurposed from industrial machinery, were used to create temporary diversions, drawing patrols away from scavenging parties.

The psychological toll of this relentless, airborne war was immense. The constant threat from above bred a deep-seated paranoia. Every distant hum of wings could trigger a panicked flight response. The very concept of open skies became a source of profound anxiety, a terrifying reminder of humanity's newfound vulnerability. Sleep became a luxury, often interrupted by the omnipresent buzz that seemed to seep into every crevice of existence. Yet, even in the face of such overwhelming despair, the flicker of resistance remained. The development of these desperate countermeasures, while often crude and ethically questionable, represented humanity's refusal to surrender. Each deployment, each experiment, each successful evasion was a small victory in a war that was far from over, a testament to the indomitable will of a species pushed to the brink, fighting for every last breath under a sky that had become a battlefield.

The buzzing, the incessant, maddening thrum that had become the soundtrack to humanity's twilight, was not a chaotic cacophony. Beneath the surface of sheer, overwhelming numbers, there pulsed a rhythm, a deeply ingrained order that belied the apparent frenzy. It was the sound of an alliance, forged not in treaties or mutual benefit as humans understood them, but in the primal, absolute imperative of survival. Each species, each caste, each individual drone, no matter how alien its form or function, contributed to a unified purpose, a singular drive that held the vast, terrifying insectoid collective together against the desperate, scattered efforts of mankind.

Consider the colossal, chitinous behemoths, the walking fortresses that lumbered across the ravaged landscapes. Their sheer mass and brute strength were formidable, capable of leveling entire city blocks with a single, earth-shattering stomp. Yet, they were not merely unthinking engines of destruction. When they advanced, smaller, winged scouts, iridescent scarabs the size of predatory birds, would flit ahead, their multifaceted eyes scanning for threats, their antennae twitching, relaying vital information back to the lumbering titans. These scouts, far more vulnerable, acted as the eyes and ears for their larger brethren, identifying potential ambush points, guiding them around collapsed infrastructure, and signaling the presence of human resistance. The titans, in turn, provided a mobile shield for the more delicate species, offering a buffer against the increasingly desperate, albeit futile, ground-based attacks humanity mounted. Their slow, deliberate movements were punctuated by moments of unexpected agility, not from their own volition, but from the subtle, almost imperceptible nudges and directions provided by the aerial swarm, a silent symphony of guidance and protection.

THE NEW DAWN

The cacophony of the insectoid advance had long been the defining sound of humanity's grim new reality. It was a symphony of clicks, screeches, and the ceaseless, maddening thrum that pulsed through the very earth. Yet, beneath the veneer of chaotic aggression, a chillingly sophisticated order had begun to reveal itself, an alliance forged in the crucible of mutual survival, far removed from any human understanding of diplomacy or shared benefit. The sheer scale of their coordinated offensives, the almost sentient understanding of battlefield tactics displayed by species that had, by all accounts, evolved in isolated ecosystems, spoke of a unified purpose, a single, terrifying drive that held the disparate insectoid castes together against the increasingly desperate, fragmented efforts of mankind.

Consider the colossal, chitinous behemoths, the walking fortresses that lumbered across the ravaged landscapes, their sheer mass and brute strength capable of leveling entire city blocks with a single, earth-shattering stomp. They were not merely unthinking engines of destruction. When they advanced, smaller, winged scouts, iridescent scarabs the size of predatory birds, would flit ahead, their multifaceted eyes scanning for threats, their antennae twitching, relaying vital information back to the lumbering titans. These scouts, far more vulnerable, acted as the eyes and ears for their larger brethren, identifying potential ambush points, guiding them around collapsed infrastructure, and signaling the presence of human resistance. The titans, in turn, provided a mobile shield for the more delicate species, offering a buffer against the increasingly desperate, albeit futile, ground-based attacks humanity mounted. Their slow, deliberate movements were punctuated by moments of unexpected agility, not from their own volition, but from the subtle, almost imperceptible nudges and directions provided by the aerial swarm, a silent symphony of guidance and protection.

Witness the aerial formations, vast, undulating carpets of wings that blotted out the sun. Within these seemingly homogenous masses, distinct species operated in concert. The primary attack units, the razor-winged raptors, were often supported by smaller, more agile flyers, akin to biological kamikaze drones. These smaller units, filled with potent, corrosive bio-fluids, would dive bomb human fortifications, their sacrifice creating breaches through which the larger, more heavily armored species could exploit. But the true genius of their coordination lay in the symbiotic relationship they fostered with the larger, slower-moving aerial carriers – gargantuan, insectoid dirigibles that drifted lazily through the upper atmosphere. These carriers, slow and heavily defended, served as mobile nutrient dispensers and reproduction hubs, launching fresh waves of attackers while also providing a vital, airborne platform for the smaller scout species. The smaller scouts, in turn, acted as mobile interceptors, preying on any human aerial assets that dared to venture into the sky, protecting the carriers from the desperate, last-ditch efforts of humanity's dwindling air forces. It was a constant, evolving ballet of predation and defense, a testament to an intelligence that understood the value of specialized roles and mutual support.

Even the subterranean dwellers, the burrowing horrors that churned the earth and undermined human strongholds, found their niche within this grand, horrific alliance. These creatures, blind and powerful, were often guided by the faint, residual sensory input from the surface-dwelling species. The vibrations of marching human columns, the subtle shifts in atmospheric pressure caused by aerial patrols, were all translated into directives that the burrowers could understand and act upon. In return for this guidance, their seismic disruption often created strategic advantages for other species. Collapsed tunnels could funnel human forces into pre-determined kill zones, their burrowing activities could destabilize structures, bringing them down upon unsuspecting defenders, and their sheer, disruptive presence often drew human attention away from more critical insectoid operations elsewhere. It was a silent, unseen coordination, a network of pressure points and strategic demolitions that served the overarching goals of the collective.

This inter-species cooperation was not born of affection or sentiment. It was a cold, calculated efficiency, a biological imperative amplified by a shared, existential threat. Humanity's desperate, often crude, attempts at countermeasures, particularly the widespread deployment of chemical agents and sonic repellents, had, ironically, served to further solidify the insectoid alliance. The rapid development of resistance to certain chemical compounds, while a setback for humanity, had spurred a rapid sharing of genetic information and adaptation strategies across different insectoid species. A species that developed a particular immunity or a method to counteract a specific sonic frequency would, through means still not fully understood by human scientists, disseminate that knowledge, that adaptation, throughout the collective. It was a biological internet, an evolutionary arms race where the speed of adaptation was paramount, and where every successful adaptation was a shared victory, a collective hardening against the encroaching tide of human desperation.

The sheer diversity of the insectoid species, which humanity initially viewed as a weakness, a fragmented multitude of disparate threats, proved to be its greatest strength. While human efforts focused on developing a single, overarching weapon or strategy, the insectoid alliance possessed an inherent adaptability stemming from its varied biological makeup. A strategy that failed against one species might be devastatingly effective against another, and the collective's ability to learn and adapt from these varied encounters meant that their overall learning curve was exponentially steeper. The discovery of a chemical that disrupted the neural pathways of the larger, armored ground units could be integrated into the attack vectors against smaller, flying scouts by altering delivery mechanisms and target parameters. The sonic frequencies that disoriented the wing-beats of one species could be modified to disrupt the vibrational communication of the subterranean dwellers.

There were instances, observed by the few surviving human reconnaissance units that dared to venture close to insectoid strongholds, that illustrated this profound solidarity. A swarm of smaller, wasp-like insects, notorious for their paralyzing sting, were observed defending a cluster of eggs belonging to a much larger, more vulnerable species, shielding them from a desperate human scavenging party. The wasp-like insects, outnumbered and outmatched in raw power, fought with a ferocity that defied their individual fragility, their synchronized attacks, their venomous precision, holding back the human assault until larger, more formidable guardians arrived. In another observed incident, during a coordinated human artillery barrage aimed at a primary insectoid congregation point, a contingent of the giant, beetle-like ground units, normally focused on their own destructive path, had altered their course, positioning their massive bodies to shield a section of the swarm's aerial transit routes from the incoming fire. It was not a tactical repositioning for their own benefit; it was a deliberate, sacrificial act of defense for the collective.

The sheer biological efficiency of the insectoid alliance was a grim marvel. Their reproduction rates were astronomical, their ability to adapt to environmental changes unparalleled, and their lack of internal conflict, at least as humans understood it, meant that their energy and resources were perpetually directed outwards, towards the singular goal of eliminating the human threat. There were no political factions, no resource disputes, no ideological schisms to divert their attention or sap their strength. Their entire existence was a unified, relentless march towards dominion, a biological imperative that transcended the individual and embraced the entirety of the collective. Humanity, with its inherent individualism, its propensity for self-destruction, and its often-conflicting desires, found itself pitted against an enemy that embodied the very antithesis of its own nature. The alliance held firm, not through sentiment, but through the unshakeable, unwavering logic of shared survival, a biological destiny playing out on a ravaged planet.

The stark reality of the insectoid capacity for sustained, large-scale conflict had, over the preceding months, seeped into the collective consciousness of humanity not as a trickle, but as a relentless, crushing tide. Initial military assessments, born of a deeply ingrained arrogance and a desperate hope for conventional victory, had consistently underestimated the sheer adaptability and coordinated threat posed by the alien swarm. Each localized victory, each temporary pushback against a particular infestation, had been lauded as a turning point, a sign that humanity's technological and tactical superiority would ultimately prevail. These pronouncements, however, had become increasingly hollow, drowned out by the ever-present hum of the insectoid advance and the stark, undeniable evidence of their persistent, ever-expanding territorial gains. The planet was, to put it mildly, being systematically consumed.

The concept of "front lines" had dissolved into a meaningless abstraction. Human-controlled enclaves, once thought to be impregnable bastions of civilization, were now isolated islands in a vast, roiling ocean of chitin and venom. Cities that had once been symbols of human achievement were now little more than ruins, scavenged for resources by the relentless insectoid forces, or worse, repurposed as breeding grounds and staging posts for further offensives. The sheer logistical undertaking of mounting any significant counter-offensive had become an insurmountable hurdle. Every attempt to concentrate forces, to establish a defensive perimeter, was met with overwhelming, multifaceted assaults that exploited every conceivable weakness. The insectoids demonstrated an unnerving ability to identify and capitalize on human vulnerabilities, whether it was a lapse in patrol patterns, a supply chain interruption, or a simple flaw in a defensive structure.

The military high command, once a body of unyielding confidence, was now a fractured entity, grappling with the existential crisis humanity faced. The traditional strategies of attrition and overwhelming force, honed over centuries of human warfare, proved catastrophically ineffective. The insectoids did not bleed in the same way; their numbers were seemingly inexhaustible, their resilience in the face of chemical agents and kinetic weaponry bordering on the miraculous. Furthermore, their constant adaptation rendered any tactical innovation obsolete almost as soon as it was deployed. A new sonic deterrent effective against one species would be countered by another, its frequency subtly altered, its intensity modulated, until it was rendered harmless, or worse, became a tool for the insectoids themselves, perhaps disrupting human communication systems or disorienting defending forces.

It was during the agonizingly protracted siege of what remained of New Denver that the undeniable shift in strategic thinking began to solidify. The city, once a sprawling metropolis, had been reduced to a few heavily fortified sectors, its population clinging to survival by a thread. The insectoid offensive against New Denver was not a single, overwhelming wave, but a series of meticulously coordinated assaults, each targeting a different aspect of the city's defenses. First came the subterranean units, their seismic disruption weakening the foundations of perimeter walls, creating access points for the ground-based behemoths. Simultaneously, aerial swarms hammered the skies, their bio-corrosive payloads melting through reinforced plating, while smaller, agile units harassed human air defenses, forcing them to spread their limited resources thin. The defenders, outnumbered and outmaneuvered, fought with a ferocity born of desperation, but it was a losing battle against an enemy that seemed to possess an inexhaustible supply of both soldiers and strategies.

The final days of New Denver were a horrific testament to the insectoids' capacity for sustained, all-encompassing warfare. When the ground assaults finally breached the last remaining defenses, it was not a chaotic free-for-all. Instead, specialized castes moved with chilling precision. Burrowing units secured subterranean tunnels, preventing escape routes, while massive, multi-limbed insectoids systematically neutralized pockets of resistance, their movements guided by the ever-present aerial scouts. Even as the last human defenders fought their desperate, futile battles, the insectoids began the process of assimilation, their biological processes already adapting the city's infrastructure for their own purposes. The scale of the loss was immense, not just in terms of lives, but in the symbolic crushing of human resilience.

This catastrophic event, coupled with a string of similarly devastating defeats across the globe, forced a profound and deeply unwelcome re-evaluation of humanity's position. The military council, comprised of the few surviving high-ranking officers and civilian leaders, convened in a heavily guarded bunker, the air thick with the palpable despair of their situation. The usual posturing, the confident pronouncements of imminent victory, were absent. Instead, a grim silence hung heavy as they sifted through the latest casualty reports, the dwindling supply inventories, and the stark assessments of insectoid capabilities. The consensus, reached through agonizing debate and the undeniable evidence of repeated failures, was inescapable: humanity could no longer afford to view the insectoids as merely a monstrous biological threat to be eradicated through brute force. They were an organized, adaptive, and ultimately superior force on the battlefield, capable of waging a war of attrition that humanity was destined to lose.

The first, and perhaps most significant, concession was the acknowledgment that purely aggressive tactics were unsustainable. The relentless pursuit of offensive operations, the constant need to reclaim territory or destroy insectoid strongholds, was bleeding humanity dry. Resources that could have been used to fortify existing settlements, to develop more resilient infrastructure, or to sustain the civilian population, were being poured into futile attempts to push back an enemy that always seemed to re-emerge, stronger and more numerous. The idea of strategic withdrawal, once considered a sign of weakness and defeatism, began to gain traction as a necessary measure of self-preservation. Certain heavily infested zones, areas where human presence was no longer tenable and any attempt to re-establish control would result in catastrophic losses, were to be declared lost. This was not surrender, the advocates argued, but a pragmatic reallocation of forces, a regrouping to preserve what remained of humanity.

This difficult decision necessitated a fundamental shift in resource allocation and strategic focus. The emphasis moved from offensive operations to consolidation and fortification. Existing human settlements were to be reinforced, their defenses bolstered with whatever technology and materials could be salvaged. Mass evacuations from outlying areas to more defensible, albeit smaller, enclaves became a priority. The goal was no longer to win back the planet, but to survive long enough to find a way to adapt, to evolve, or perhaps, to simply endure.

The notion of "diplomatic overtures" began to surface in hushed tones within the highest echelons of command. It was a concept that bordered on the sacrilegious, a betrayal of every principle humanity had fought for. To even consider negotiating with the insectoid collective, with creatures that had demonstrated such utter contempt for human life, seemed an act of utter madness. Yet, the brutal logic of survival whispered a more compelling argument. If the insectoids were indeed capable of such sophisticated coordination and adaptation, then perhaps, just perhaps, they possessed a form of intelligence that could, under certain circumstances, engage in something akin to communication. The hope, however faint, was that understanding their motivations, their needs, or even their vulnerabilities, might offer an alternative to the agonizing path of annihilation.

This radical departure from established doctrine sparked fierce debate. Many argued that any attempt at communication would be seen as a sign of weakness, an invitation for further exploitation. Others believed that the insectoids were purely instinct-driven, incapable of any form of reasoned discourse. However, a growing faction, weary of the endless bloodshed and acutely aware of humanity's dwindling reserves, began to champion the idea. They pointed to the observed patterns of insectoid behavior – the seemingly organized territorial expansions, the avoidance of certain environmental factors, the specific targeting of human infrastructure – as potential indicators of underlying objectives that might, in theory, be addressed. The proposal was not to offer terms of surrender, but to explore the possibility of co-existence, of establishing boundaries, however precarious, that could allow humanity a chance to rebuild and perhaps, in time, to understand its alien adversary. The "Great Recalibration," as it came to be known, was not a victory, but a profound and humbling concession to a reality that humanity had, for too long, refused to acknowledge.

It was the stark, terrifying realization that the war for survival had irrevocably changed, and that humanity, for the first time in its history, was no longer the undisputed apex predator on its own world. The aggressive, unrelenting pursuit of extermination had failed, and in its place, a desperate, unprecedented era of reassessment and potential appeasement had begun. The hum of the insectoid advance, once a sound of pure terror, now carried with it the unsettling resonance of a power that demanded a new, and terrifying, form of respect.

The Great Recalibration had begun, not with a triumphant roar, but with a chillingly quiet shift in perspective. The desperate scramble for survival, the entrenched dogma of eradication, had given way to a grim acknowledgment of reality. Humanity, once the master of its domain, was now a species fighting for its very existence, not through dominance, but through adaptation. The insectoid advance, once perceived as a purely destructive force, was slowly revealing a more complex, and perhaps more profound, aspect of its nature. It was a nature intrinsically linked to the scarred earth, a silent testament to an ancient pact between biology and the planet that predated human dominion.

As the initial shockwaves of defeat subsided, and the painful process of strategic withdrawal commenced, observations began to trickle in, not from the front lines of battle, but from the periphery of human comprehension. These were not reports of overwhelming aggression, but of subtle, almost benevolent, interventions. In the desolate, chemical-scarred wastelands that had once been fertile farmlands, an entirely new drama was unfolding. The air, thick with the lingering stench of decades of relentless pesticide use, was beginning to change. It was a change initiated not by human efforts – for humanity's attempts at remediation had been woefully inadequate and often exacerbated the problem – but by the very creatures that had driven them into their fortified enclaves.

Consider the vast, ochre plains that had been rendered barren by aerial spraying, the very soil poisoned to the point of sterility. Now, across these desolate expanses, a different kind of movement was taking place. Tiny, almost insignificant-looking beetles, their carapaces a dull, earthy brown, were emerging from the poisoned earth. They were not the monstrous, chitinous warriors of the battlefield, but specialized scavengers, biological janitors tasked with a monumental, and seemingly impossible, duty. These particular insectoids possessed a unique digestive system, capable of processing and neutralizing the complex chemical compounds that had rendered the land uninhabitable. They would burrow into the contaminated soil, consuming the toxic residues, their internal biological processes breaking down the harmful agents into inert byproducts. It was a slow, arduous process, measured in generations, but it was a process that was, undeniably, happening.

Witness the swarms of myrmecine ants, their colonies, once thought to be purely for propagation and defense, now engaging in intricate terraforming operations. In areas where aggressive deforestation had stripped the land bare, leading to severe soil erosion, these ants were meticulously re-establishing the natural order. They would carry seeds, often those of hardy, pioneer plants, deep into the soil, creating micro-habitats for new growth. Their tunneling activities aerated the earth, improving drainage and allowing for greater moisture retention. It was a stark contrast to the destructive burrowing that human forces had to contend with; this was an act of creation, of slow, deliberate reconstruction. Entire hillsides, once prone to landslides, were being stabilized by the intricate, interconnected networks of their subterranean cities.

The air, too, was undergoing a transformation. In regions devastated by industrial pollution, where toxic fumes had choked the skies for years, specialized winged insectoids were beginning to appear. These creatures, with their iridescent, almost crystalline wings, seemed to possess the ability to filter atmospheric pollutants. They would fly in intricate patterns, their wing membranes acting as biological air purifiers, absorbing particulate matter and neutralizing certain gaseous compounds. The effect was subtle at first, a mere lessening of the acrid bite in the air, but over time, in localized areas, the skies were clearing, revealing a hue of blue not seen in generations.

Perhaps the most striking example of this environmental reclamation was observed in the ruined urban centers. Once teeming with human life, these metropolises were now skeletal remains, monuments to humanity's hubris and its ultimate failure. Yet, even here, life, in its most resilient form, was finding a way. Vines, thick and tenacious, were beginning to snake their way up the cracked facades of skyscrapers, their roots finding purchase in the rubble. These were not ordinary plants; they were species that had been genetically engineered, or perhaps had naturally evolved, to thrive in the presence of decaying organic matter and residual chemical traces. And guiding their growth, nurturing their spread, were species of insectoid pollinators, their purpose no longer tied to the sustenance of human agriculture, but to the re-establishment of the planet's own flora.

There were reports of small, bioluminescent fungi, cultivated by specialized burrowing insectoids, that were actively breaking down petroleum-based waste and other man-made contaminants. These fungi, thriving in the darkness of subterranean ruins, were slowly but surely detoxifying the very foundations of human civilization, rendering them safe for a new, burgeoning ecosystem. The insectoids, in this context, were not the destroyers, but the architects of a nascent rebirth. They were not driven by any discernible malice towards humanity, but by an intrinsic biological imperative to restore balance, to heal the wounds inflicted upon the planet, wounds that humanity, in its destructive ambition, had so carelessly inflicted.

This revelation forced a profound re-evaluation of the entire conflict. The insectoids were not a singular, monolithic entity driven by a singular desire for human annihilation. Instead, they represented a vast, interconnected web of life, each species playing a role in a grander, ecological drama. The aggressive military castes, the ones humanity had so readily demonized, were merely one facet of this multifaceted collective. There were others, the silent laborers, the patient healers, the tireless cultivators, whose efforts were directed not towards conquest, but towards restoration.

The implications of this discovery were staggering. If the insectoids were, in essence, attempting to heal the planet, what did that say about humanity's role in this new world order? Had humanity become the invasive species, the blight that needed to be eradicated not out of hatred, but out of necessity for the planet's own survival? The idea was anathema to everything humanity believed about itself, yet the evidence was becoming increasingly difficult to ignore. The planet, once a canvas for human ambition, was now actively resisting its former masters, and the insectoids, in their alien way, were its immune system.

The scientists and xenobiologists, those few who had survived and were now operating in the highly protected research enclaves, began to meticulously document these environmental restoration efforts. They observed how certain insectoid species would actively dismantle and re-purpose human-made structures, not for combat, but for the creation of new habitats. Metal alloys were broken down into their constituent elements, concrete was pulverized and incorporated into new soil compositions, and plastics, the persistent plague of human waste, were being consumed by specialized, enzyme-secreting organisms. It was a process of planetary recycling on an unimaginable scale, a slow, deliberate undoing of humanity's environmental footprint.

One particular observation involved a species of immense, millipede-like creatures, their segmented bodies stretching for hundreds of feet. These behemoths, previously feared for their ability to collapse tunnels and destabilize fortifications, were now seen traversing vast swathes of contaminated land. They would consume entire layers of poisoned soil, their passage leaving behind a trail of rejuvenated earth, teeming with the nascent life of hardy microorganisms and resilient plant spores. It was as if the planet itself was breathing again, exhaling the toxins and inhaling a new beginning, guided by the silent, relentless labor of its alien caretakers.

The implications for human strategy were immense. If the insectoid collective was driven by a need to restore ecological balance, then humanity's continued existence as a disruptive force was fundamentally at odds with their goals. This did not necessarily mean that direct conflict was their only recourse. Perhaps, just perhaps, there was a possibility for understanding, for finding a niche, however small, within this newly emerging ecological paradigm. The idea of co-existence, once a fantastical notion dismissed as preposterous, was now being considered with a desperate, pragmatic urgency.

The question remained: how could humanity negotiate with a force that operated on such fundamentally different biological and perhaps even philosophical principles? Their motivations were not rooted in greed, or conquest in the human sense, but in an instinctual, profound connection to the planet itself. They were, in a way, extensions of the Earth's will, its antibodies rising to combat a pervasive infection. Humanity, therefore, had to fundamentally alter its perception of the enemy, not as a horde of mindless monsters, but as a manifestation of the planet's own survival instinct.

The recalibration was more than just a strategic shift; it was an existential reckoning. Humanity had to confront the uncomfortable truth that its dominance had come at a terrible cost, a cost the planet was now actively rectifying. The seeds of a new ecosystem were being sown, not by human hands, but by the very forces that had sought to overwhelm them. And within this burgeoning new world, humanity's future, if it had one at all, would be defined not by its ability to conquer, but by its capacity to adapt, to integrate, and perhaps, to finally learn to live in harmony with the planet it had so brutally exploited. The insectoids were not just warriors; they were gardeners, tending to a world that had been ravaged by a careless hand, preparing the soil for a future that excluded, or at least severely limited, the presence of its former stewards. The silent work of restoration continued, a constant, unfolding testament to a planetary resilience that humanity had long since forgotten.

The cacophony of war, once the relentless soundtrack to humanity's desperate existence, had begun to fade, replaced by a more unsettling quiet. It was the quiet of observation, of introspection, and of a dawning, terrifying realization. The Great Recalibration wasn't just a shift in military tactics; it was a seismic upheaval in the very definition of humanity's place on Earth. For generations, survival had been synonymous with dominance, with the eradication of anything that threatened the human species. Now, the insectoids, the very embodiment of that threat, were revealing a capacity for something entirely unexpected: a profound, almost paternalistic stewardship of the planet. This revelation cast a long shadow over every salvaged outpost, every huddled community. The war hadn't ended in victory or defeat, but in a weary pause, a moment where the survivors looked at their scarred world and saw not just ruins, but the nascent stirrings of an alien renewal.

Within the reinforced bunkers and the hastily erected

geodesic domes, the initial shock gave way to a hesitant pragmatism. The xenobiologists, their faces etched with exhaustion and a dawning wonder, presented their findings with a gravity that silenced even the most hardened soldiers. The insectoids weren't a singular force of destruction. They were an ecosystem, a complex, interconnected network dedicated to planetary healing. Their seemingly random acts of aggression were, in many instances, precise interventions, the biological equivalent of pruning diseased branches to save a vital tree. Humanity, it seemed, had become the disease.

The implications were as profound as they were disorienting. If the insectoids were the planet's immune system, then humanity was the pathogen. This wasn't a matter of good versus evil, of heroes and villains. It was a matter of biological necessity. The very actions that had secured human dominance – the strip-mining, the deforestation, the unchecked industrial pollution – had pushed the planet to the brink. And the insectoids, in their alien, instinctual way, were the world's desperate attempt to survive humanity's reign.

This new understanding necessitated a radical shift in strategy, a move away from outright annihilation towards something far more delicate and fraught with peril: coexistence. The idea was met with a spectrum of reactions, from outright derision to a desperate, flickering hope. Many still saw the insectoids as monstrous threats, their current 'restorative' actions merely a prelude to a more targeted extermination of humanity. Others, those who had witnessed firsthand the silent, tireless work of the insectoid laborers, began to consider the unthinkable. Could humanity negotiate with a species that communicated through pheromones and vibrational frequencies, a species whose entire societal structure was alien beyond comprehension?

The first tentative steps towards de-escalation were taken

in the peripheral zones, areas where human settlements had been less aggressively contested. These were often regions already heavily influenced by insectoid ecological management, where the air was cleaner, the soil was slowly regenerating, and the scars of human exploitation were beginning to fade. It was in these zones that the impossible began to take shape. Small, isolated human enclaves, stripped of their offensive capabilities and reduced to a state of vulnerable observation, found themselves in a strange détente with the insectoid forces that patrolled their immediate vicinities.

These weren't formal treaties signed with ink on parchment. They were tacit agreements, unspoken understandings forged in the crucible of mutual survival. For instance, the sprawling agricultural domes, once gleaming fortresses of human ingenuity, now operated under a fragile truce. Insectoid species, specifically those designated as 'pollinators' and 'soil enrichers' by xenobiologists, would skirt the perimeter of these domes, their presence a constant, silent reminder of the new order. Any attempt by humans to expand beyond the designated perimeters, to reassert dominance over the surrounding, regenerating landscape, was met not with overwhelming force, but with precisely targeted disruptions. Swarms of smaller insectoids would meticulously dismantle any new construction, their actions methodical and efficient, leaving behind no immediate threat but a clear message.

The 'negotiations' were indirect, relying on observation and cautious experimentation. Human scientists, working from secure observation posts, would carefully monitor the insectoid response to specific actions. If a dome's waste management system malfunctioned, releasing toxic runoff into the newly purified waterways, the insectoid response was swift. Not a full-scale assault, but a localized concentration of 'cleaner' insectoids that would effectively contain the spill, their biological processes neutralizing the toxins. It was a stark lesson in responsibility, delivered without a single audible word.

This led to the development of entirely new protocols for human interaction with the insectoid world. Resource acquisition, once a matter of conquest, now involved a complex dance of understanding ecological limits. Certain minerals, vital for sustaining human technology, were found in areas designated by insectoid activity as critical regeneration zones. Harvesting these minerals would inevitably disrupt the delicate balance the insectoids were working to restore. The choice was stark: abandon the resource, or risk a devastating, albeit localized, retaliation.

The concept of 'boundaries' became paramount. Through painstaking observation, scientists began to map out the territories of different insectoid species and their specific roles in planetary restoration. It became evident that certain regions were vital for the life cycles of specific insectoid castes, serving as nurseries for larvae, breeding grounds, or migratory pathways. Entering these zones was akin to trespassing on sacred ground. The insectoids, while not exhibiting overt aggression, would employ non-lethal deterrents – sonic frequencies, pheromonal clouds that induced disorientation, or even targeted physical barriers formed by specialized burrowing species.

One particularly challenging negotiation involved the salvaged remnants of a pre-Collapse hydroelectric dam. The dam was a crucial source of power for a significant human population cluster. However, the surrounding river, once choked with industrial pollutants, was now teeming with aquatic insectoid species that were slowly but surely detoxifying the water. These creatures, some resembling giant, phosphorescent crustaceans, played a vital role in filtering and processing the residual chemicals. The humans needed the dam's power, but restarting its turbines would disrupt the river's ecosystem, potentially harming the aquatic insectoids and reversing years of painstaking natural remediation.

The solution, arrived at after months of observation and cautious testing, was a compromise. The dam's operation would be drastically scaled back, generating only enough power to sustain essential life support systems for the human settlement. Furthermore, a complex filtration system, designed in collaboration with xenobiologists who studied the insectoids' own filtering mechanisms, was installed upstream. This system mimicked the biological processes of the aquatic insectoids, creating a parallel purification stream that allowed the river's natural detoxifiers to continue their work unimpeded. It was a fragile, technologically dependent peace, a testament to humanity's newfound humility.

The political landscape within the human enclaves also underwent a transformation. The old power structures, built on military might and resource control, crumbled. New leadership emerged, comprised of individuals who possessed not just resilience, but also an understanding of the new ecological realities. Xenobiologists, ecologists, and even those with a background in diplomacy – albeit with an alien species – found themselves at the forefront of decision-making. The 'Great Recalibration' demanded a new kind of leader, one who could negotiate with the planet itself, through its insectoid custodians.

The greatest hurdle remained the sheer alienness of the insectoid collective. There was no common language, no shared history, no discernible hierarchy in the human sense. Their motivations were biological imperatives, their communication channels fundamentally different. Yet, through meticulous, painstaking observation, patterns began to emerge. Certain insectoid species showed a marked preference for specific regions, actively defending them against the encroachment of other, less beneficial species, including any aberrant human activities. This suggested a form of territoriality, an instinct to protect and nurture specific ecosystems.

Scientists hypothesized that if they could identify and respect these 'managed territories,' they might be able to carve out their own safe zones. It was a delicate dance of learning to read the subtle cues of the insectoid world. A sudden flurry of activity by burrowing insects might signal an area undergoing deep soil remediation, rendering it temporarily unstable. A congregation of winged insectoids with iridescent wings could indicate a particularly sensitive atmospheric purification process underway. Ignoring these cues, attempting to force human will upon these natural rhythms, invariably led to swift, albeit often non-lethal, correction.

The notion of 'mutual respect' was the fragile cornerstone of this new order. For humanity, it meant acknowledging that their existence was no longer paramount. They were a species that had profoundly wounded its host planet, and the insectoids were the Earth's way of healing. Respecting the insectoids meant respecting the planet's own recovery. For the insectoids, the manifestation of this respect was the absence of direct, overwhelming hostility in many zones. They didn't seek to exterminate humanity, provided humanity remained within its designated, limited sphere of influence and did not actively impede the planet's regeneration.

The most challenging aspect of these nascent negotiations was the very definition of 'sentience' and 'intelligence.' Were the insectoids consciously making these decisions? Or were they merely acting on ingrained biological programming? The answer, most scientists agreed, was likely a complex blend of both. They possessed an intelligence that operated on a planetary scale, a distributed consciousness woven into the very fabric of the ecosystem. Humanity, accustomed to individualistic thought and complex abstract reasoning, struggled to comprehend a form of sentience that was so fundamentally collective and biologically driven.

Despite the immense challenges, the fragile truces held. In certain carefully managed agricultural zones, humans cultivated nutrient-rich crops under the watchful, silent presence of insectoid guardians. These guardians, often colossal, armored beetles, would patrol the perimeter, their sheer size and resilience deterring any potential threats – mutated fauna, desperate raiders, or even careless human expansion. Their presence, once terrifying, now served as an odd sort of reassurance, a sign that the immediate vicinity was considered 'stable' by the planet's primary custodians.

The ongoing efforts to establish clear boundaries extended to the salvaged technological remnants of the old world. Abandoned cities, once teeming with life and now skeletal ruins, were clearly delineated. Certain sectors, particularly those containing hazardous waste or unstable structures, were designated as 'no-go zones' for humans, actively patrolled and, in some cases, physically altered by insectoid forces to prevent human access. Other areas, deemed ecologically inert or already undergoing a form of managed decay, were grudgingly left to the remaining human populations, provided they adhered to strict waste disposal and resource management protocols.

The 'New Dawn' was not a return to the past, nor was it a triumphant conquest of the future. It was a tentative, hesitant dawn, painted with the muted colors of compromise and the stark reality of interdependence. Humanity, stripped of its arrogance and its illusion of absolute control, was learning to live in the shadow of a new planetary order. The insectoids, once perceived as an existential threat, were slowly revealing themselves as the unintended architects of humanity's survival, not through benevolent intent, but through the cold, unyielding logic of ecological balance. The future would not be built on human dominance, but on a precarious, hard-won understanding with the very forces that had almost extinguished them. The fragile truce was not a peace treaty, but a shared breath in a world that was slowly, irrevocably, healing itself.

The echoes of the Great Recalibration were more than just the receding sounds of conflict; they were ingrained in the very fabric of existence. Humanity, once the undisputed apex predator, had been humbled, its arrogance systematically dismantled by an enemy that proved to be not an enemy at all, but a force of nature, a planet's desperate immune response. The war, brutal and all-consuming, had ended not with a bang, but with a whisper – the quiet, persistent hum of insectoid labor restoring the ravaged earth. This new dawn was not a celebration of victory, but a somber reckoning with the profound and irreversible consequences of generations of environmental neglect and the predatory instinct that had defined humanity for too long.

The lesson was stark and unforgiving: the Earth was not a boundless resource to be exploited, but a complex, interconnected organism. Humanity had treated it like a disposable commodity, a canvas upon which to paint its ambitions, heedless of the biological ecosystems it was systematically destroying. The strip-mining that scarred continents, the deforestation that annihilated vital carbon sinks, the unchecked industrial pollution that poisoned air and water – these were not mere acts of progress, but acts of self-mutilation. The insectoids, in their alien, instinctual wisdom, had simply been the planet's antibodies, a biological mechanism to purge the infestation. And humanity, it turned out, had been the ultimate pathogen.

This realization was a bitter pill to swallow. For so long, survival had been synonymous with dominance, with the eradication of anything that posed a perceived threat. The insectoids, with their terrifying swarm tactics and their seemingly insatiable drive, had been the ultimate manifestation of that threat. Yet, in their current role as planetary custodians, they displayed a remarkable capacity for restoration, for meticulous, tireless work that aimed not at destruction, but at healing. It was a paradigm shift so radical, so disorienting, that it fractured the collective human psyche. Many clung to the old narratives, labeling the insectoids' actions as a temporary lull before a final, decisive extermination. Others, those who had witnessed the silent, tireless work of the insectoid 'gardeners' and 'purifiers,' began to see a flicker of possibility in the ashes of their former world: the possibility of coexistence.

The war had stripped humanity bare, not just of its infrastructure and advanced weaponry, but of its hubris. The salvaged outposts, the huddling survivors in reinforced bunkers and geodesic domes, were testaments to their resilience, but also to their profound vulnerability. Their technological might, once the bedrock of their perceived supremacy, now seemed like a childish bluster against the patient, inexorable forces of planetary regeneration. The very air they breathed, once a privilege, was now a meticulously managed resource, its quality a direct reflection of their adherence to the new, unspoken rules dictated by their alien custodians.

The memory of the insect war was a phantom limb, a constant, aching reminder of what had been lost and what could have been prevented. Every sunrise, painting the sky with hues of crimson and gold against the backdrop of slowly recovering landscapes, served as a visual epitaph to their past recklessness. The clean rivers, where phosphorescent aquatic insectoids now patrolled their depths, were a stark contrast to the toxic, stagnant waterways of yesteryear. The forests, where specialized insectoid castes meticulously tended to saplings and cleared diseased flora, stood as silent witnesses to the centuries of human deforestation.

This was not a history to be forgotten, but a history to be learned from. The survivors understood, with a clarity born of utter devastation, that the concept of 'human exceptionalism' was a dangerous delusion. They were but one species among billions, and their survival was contingent upon their ability to integrate themselves back into the planet's intricate web of life, rather than attempting to dominate it. The insectoids, in their inscrutable way, had enforced this fundamental truth. Their presence was a perpetual sermon on the interconnectedness of all living things.

The agricultural domes, once symbols of human ingenuity and control over nature, now operated under a fragile, unspoken truce. The colossal, armored beetles that patrolled their perimeters were not merely deterrents against external threats; they were living embodiments of the new ecological contract. Their sheer, silent presence was a constant, visceral reminder of humanity's diminished status. Any deviation from the prescribed boundaries, any hint of a return to old habits of expansion or resource hoarding, was met with precise, targeted interventions. Swarms of smaller, specialized insectoids would meticulously dismantle unauthorized construction, their efficiency unnerving, their message clear: respect the boundaries, or face the consequences.

The xenobiologists, the unsung heroes of this new era, became the translators of the insectoid world. Their days were consumed by the painstaking, meticulous observation of pheromone trails, vibrational frequencies, and subtle shifts in insectoid behavior. They learned to read the planet's ecological pulse through its insectoid custodians. A sudden surge of burrowing activity indicated an area undergoing deep soil remediation, rendering it temporarily unstable and off-limits to human passage. A congregation of winged insectoids with iridescent wings signaled an atmospheric purification process underway, a delicate operation that could be easily disrupted. These were not mere observations; they were vital directives, the language of survival spoken in the silent, complex dialect of biology.

The ethical dilemmas were profound. The idea of negotiating with a species so fundamentally alien, whose motivations were rooted in biological imperatives rather than abstract reasoning, was a concept that stretched the very definition of sentience. Were the insectoids conscious in the human sense? Or were they merely automatons, programmed by an ancient, planetary intelligence? The prevailing scientific consensus leaned towards a complex intermingling of both: an emergent intelligence, a distributed consciousness woven into the very fabric of the ecosystem, acting in unison for the planet's well-being.

This understanding demanded a fundamental redefinition of human purpose. No longer were they the architects of their own destiny, charting a course of technological advancement and territorial expansion. Now, they were caretakers, stewards, their role reduced to that of a single, vital component within a vastly larger, more complex system. Their ingenuity was not directed towards conquering nature, but towards understanding and integrating with it. Their technological prowess was repurposed for environmental monitoring, for developing bio-mimetic systems that replicated insectoid functions, for creating symbiotic technologies that could aid, rather than harm, the planet's healing process.

The salvaged remnants of the old world – the skeletal cities, the rusting hulks of forgotten machinery – served as a constant visual reminder of humanity's past follies. These ruins were not merely historical sites; they were ecological hazards, clearly delineated zones that the insectoids actively patrolled and, in some cases, physically altered to prevent human access. Areas containing hazardous waste or unstable structures were marked as 'no-go zones,' enforced by specialized insectoid castes whose sole purpose was to contain and neutralize lingering toxins. Conversely, sectors deemed ecologically inert or already undergoing a process of managed decay were grudgingly left to the remaining human populations, with the strict caveat that they adhere to rigorous waste disposal and resource management protocols.

The Great Recalibration had, in essence, initiated a planetary rebalancing. Humanity's attempt to impose its will upon the Earth had failed spectacularly, leading to a near-apocalyptic collapse. The insectoids, by fulfilling their ecological imperative, had inadvertently become the saviors of the very species that had threatened their existence. This was not a saviordom born of altruism, but of biological necessity. The planet, like any living organism, would defend itself against the forces that threatened its integrity.

The consequences of this radical recalibration were woven into the daily lives of the survivors. Resource acquisition, once a matter of conquest and control, now involved a complex dance of understanding ecological limits. Certain minerals, vital for maintaining the salvaged technologies that sustained human life, were located in areas designated by insectoid activity as critical regeneration zones. Harvesting these resources would inevitably disrupt the delicate ecological balance the insectoids were working to restore. The choice was stark: abandon the resource, or risk a swift, albeit localized, retaliation. This led to the development of sophisticated resource management systems, prioritizing sustainability and minimizing impact. Recycling and repurposing salvaged materials became not just an economic necessity, but an ethical imperative.

The concept of 'boundaries' was no longer a political or territorial construct, but an ecological one. Through painstaking observation, scientists began to map out the territories of different insectoid species and their specific roles in planetary restoration. It became evident that certain regions were vital for the life cycles of specific insectoid castes, serving as nurseries for larvae, breeding grounds, or migratory pathways. Entering these zones was akin to trespassing on sacred ground, an act of profound disrespect that would invariably be met with non-lethal deterrents – sonic frequencies that induced disorientation, pheromonal clouds that triggered intense anxiety, or even targeted physical barriers formed by specialized burrowing species.

The long-term consequences of the conflict were not simply about rebuilding what had been destroyed. They were about fundamentally transforming humanity's relationship with its planet and its inhabitants. The memory of the insect war served as a constant, sobering reminder of their vulnerability. It was a visceral understanding of the fact that they were not the masters of the Earth, but rather one species among many, reliant on the planet's health for their own survival. The insectoids, once perceived as an existential threat, had evolved in the human consciousness to become the ultimate symbol of nature's resilience and power.

The new dawn was painted with the muted colors of compromise and the stark reality of interdependence. Humanity, stripped of its arrogance and its illusion of absolute control, was learning to live in the shadow of a new planetary order. The future would not be built on human dominance, but on a precarious, hard-won understanding with the very forces that had almost extinguished them. The fragile truce was not a peace treaty, but a shared breath in a world that was slowly, irrevocably, healing itself. The echoes of the past were a constant, low hum, a reminder of the devastating repercussions of environmental irresponsibility, and a testament to the enduring, vital necessity of a more sustainable coexistence with nature. They were learning, slowly and painfully, that the Earth's healing was their only hope, and that the insectoids were its dedicated, unwavering healers. Their existence, their continued survival, depended on respecting the intricate tapestry of life that the insectoids were diligently, and silently, reweaving. The war had been a crucible, and from its fires, a new, more humble humanity was beginning to emerge, forever changed by the echoes of its own near-destruction and the alien hands that had guided its hesitant return to balance.

www.ingramcontent.com/pod-product-compliance
Lightning Source LLC
Chambersburg PA
CBHW060125260626
47160CB00005B/2020